Praise for

— LOLA BENKO, —
TREASURE HUNTER

"Three heads are better than one, and these whiz kids make STEM cool as they outmaneuver the mysterious Shadow for the stone. . . . An accessible, colorful romp that ends with an alluring hint of another treasure hunt to come."

—KIRKUS REVIEWS

ALSO BY BETH MCMULLEN

MRS. SMITH'S SPY SCHOOL FOR GIRLS

#1: MRS. SMITH'S SPY SCHOOL FOR GIRLS

#2: POWER PLAY

#3: DOUBLE CROSS

LOLA BENKO, TREASURE HUNTER

#1: LOLA BENKO, TREASURE HUNTER

#2: THE MIDNIGHT MARKET

LOLA BENKO,
TREASURE HUNTER

By Beth McMullen

ALADDIN
NEW YORK   LONDON   TORONTO   SYDNEY   NEW DELHI

ALADDIN

An imprint of Simon & Schuster Children's Publishing Division
1230 Avenue of the Americas, New York, New York 10020
First Aladdin paperback edition August 2021
Text copyright © 2020 by Beth McMullen
Cover illustration copyright © 2020 by Fiona Hsieh
Also available in an Aladdin hardcover edition
All rights reserved, including the right of reproduction in whole or in part in any form.
ALADDIN and related logo are registered trademarks of Simon & Schuster, Inc.
For information about special discounts for bulk purchases, please contact
Simon & Schuster Special Sales at 1-866-506-1949 or business@simonandschuster.com.
The Simon & Schuster Speakers Bureau can bring authors to your live event.
For more information or to book an event contact the Simon & Schuster Speakers Bureau
at 1-866-248-3049 or visit our website at www.simonspeakers.com.
Designed by Laura Lyn DiSiena
The text of this book was set in Chaparral Pro.
Manufactured in the United States of America 0822 OFF
10 9 8 7 6 5 4 3 2
The Library of Congress has cataloged the hardcover edition as follows:
Names: McMullen, Beth, 1969– author.
Title: Lola Benko, treasure hunter / Beth McMullen.
Description: New York : Aladdin, 2020. | Audience: Ages 9-13. |
Summary: Sent to a private school after multiple brushes with the law, twelve-year-old Lola
Benko recruits classmates to help find her archaeologist father, who disappeared while
seeking a powerful mythical stone.
Identifiers: LCCN 2020022156 (print) | LCCN 2020022157 (ebook) |
ISBN 9781534456693 (hardcover) | ISBN 9781534456716 (ebook)
Subjects: CYAC: Adventure and adventurers—Fiction. | Relics—Fiction. |
Supernatural—Fiction. | Conduct of life—Fiction. | Private schools—Fiction. |
Schools—Fiction. | Missing persons—Fiction.
Classification: LCC PZ7.1.M4644 Lol 2020 (print) | LCC PZ7.1.M4644 (ebook) |
DDC [Fic]—dc23
LC record available at https://lccn.loc.gov/2020022156
LC ebook record available at https://lccn.loc.gov/2020022157
ISBN 9781534456709 (paperback)

For my brother, David Von Ancken. Fight on. Never quit.

LOLA BENKO,
TREASURE HUNTER

CHAPTER 1

EIGHT MONTHS AGO— PRAGUE, CZECH REPUBLIC

FROM THE OUTSIDE, MY LIFE PROBABLY LOOKS pretty good. I travel around the world with my archaeologist father searching for lost things. Not like misplaced keys or that library book you swear you returned. No, Professor Lawrence Benko is a *treasure hunter*. You know, Montezuma's gold or the plunder of the dreaded pirate Blackbeard. *That* kind of stuff. Last year we spent four months searching for the priceless Sword of Honjo Masamune, lost during World War II. The search turned out to be a wild-goose chase and a total bust. But every once in a while, the esteemed professor *finds* what he's looking for. That's when you read about him in the news or see him on television.

So what is traipsing around the world after my dad *really* like? Well, at twelve years old, I live out of a suitcase and have extra pages stapled into my passport because I used up the regular ones. I've been on all the continents except for Antarctica, and that is only because there are not many treasures buried in the ice. I've been to eleven schools in seven years, which means I know kids all over the world, but I have no *real* friends because who wants a friend who just ups and leaves at the drop of a hat? I learned to read on a boat traveling down the Mekong Delta and to divide fractions on an archaeological dig in Mali.

Dad says I'm a tinkerer. My current specialty is whirligig wind spinners made from tin cans, wire, and springs. The tinkering comes from having lots of idle time moving from place to place. When my father is in hot pursuit of some missing thing or another and 100 percent focused on his work, I am responsible for entertaining myself. I'm good at being alone. I barely even notice it. Not much, anyway.

For instance, right now I'm parked in a small dusty apartment that has been our home for thirteen hours. We came from Estonia and before that Bucharest. Or Istanbul? I can't remember. It all runs together. I'm staring out the window at two kids with backpacks down on the sidewalk. They are probably on their way to school. I notice them because one is laughing so hard at what the other just said, she doubles over to catch her breath. But I'm definitely *not* wondering what it would be like to have a friend who laughed at my jokes like that. No. I'm looking at the library across the street, so ornate and fancy it could be a royal palace. *That's* what I'm doing.

This morning, Dad took off to meet the archivist before the sun was even up, something urgent about old records and fairy tales. He left a note reminding me to do my homework before getting distracted by other projects. And while I appreciate his effort, this new whirligig I'm building is made from Coke cans and sparkles like a disco ball. It is *much* more interesting than equations or vocabulary lists. Also, when Dad goes into an archive or a library, he doesn't leave until they kick him out, which means I have plenty of time to do my homework before he gets back.

Except it turns out I don't. It's not even lunchtime when Dad crashes through the apartment's front door, hair wild and arms helicoptering. He's acting like he just got electrocuted. For the record, Dad and I look nothing alike. He's tall and lanky with silver hair and I'm short and solid with frizzy brown hair. His eyes are green like a cat and mine are brown like a mud puddle. Except Dad says they are flecked with gold and beautiful. Whatever.

"Lola!" Dad shouts, his eyes frantic. "Things have just taken a turn for the extraordinary!"

"They have?" I'm about to cut an important piece of Coke can, but I pause. When Dad is excited, the best solution is to wait him out. It never lasts more than three or four minutes. I put down my tin snips.

"Indeed." He's breathless, gulping at the air. "Places to go, people to see, things to do. Come on. Pack up. Time to move."

"But we *just* got here." This is a quick change of direction, even for us.

He waves me off. "I know. I know. But things are happening. Stupendous things. Unbelievable things."

Boy, he's really excited. "Stupendous" isn't an everyday word for Dad. "What are they?" I demand.

His expression falls flat. "I can't tell you." Great. Sometimes I can't get him to shut up about whatever artifact he's after and other times he's silent as the grave. Is it too much to ask for a happy medium?

"Then you shouldn't taunt me with 'stupendous' and 'unbelievable,'" I grumble.

Dad takes me by the shoulders. "I share your sorrow that we cannot stay longer in beautiful Prague, but I must take the tiger by the tail on this one. It requires a full-court press." Dad loves a good idiom, but I'm still annoyed.

Clearly he doesn't care, as he spins around the apartment, picking up the few things we've managed to unpack and hurling them into our bags. It occurs to me Dad has not asked about my homework and that is always his first question. Something strange is *definitely* going on.

"Fine. But I need an hour to take this apart." I point at the half-constructed whirligig. It's my most ambitious creation yet, and there is no way I'm going to mess it up because Dad is having some sort of unexplained meltdown. "Where are we going anyway?"

Dad eyes the three-foot whirligig with suspicion, as if seeing it for the first time. "Well, I'm headed to Budapest. But you are going to San Francisco."

I drop a coil of wire. "*Excuse* me? San Francisco?" Not that I don't like San Francisco. I love it there. I stay with Great-Aunt Irma, who is the best, and her companion gray parrot, Zeus, who's the best at being trouble. Irma always has three flavors of ice cream in the freezer and never nags me to brush my hair, although once Zeus tried to make a nest in there and I knew enough to take the hint. But the point is, Dad is dropping me like a hot potato. "Why?"

Dad flashes a pained expression. "Just for a few months."

"*Months?*"

"Weeks? Is that better? I can't say for sure, but it's a

necessary precaution," he explains. "It might not be safe."

"*What's* not safe?"

"Perhaps that's the wrong word? Well, in any case, not to worry. Everything is fine. It's just Irma would dearly love to see you and I figured now that it's almost summer, it would be a good time. Plus, I have things to do. They won't be fun for you. Very boring. Dull. Boring and dull."

"You *said* not safe."

"You misheard me. And the whirligig will have to stay."

I'm pretty good at being spontaneous. I mean, really. Look at me. But even I have my limits. "No. Way."

"You can't fly with it. It's very . . . weird." When I scowl at him, he retreats. "You know what I mean. They are picky about what you can bring on airplanes these days."

"I don't care. I'm not leaving it."

"You must."

"I refuse." I cross my arms against my chest defensively.

Dad's jaw tightens. In his head, he's reeling through strategies to get me to comply with his wishes. It won't work. He might as well give up now and save himself the time. I grimace, just in case my point is somehow unclear.

After glancing at his watch, he throws his hands up in the air. "Fine! I'll ship it to you."

I narrow my gaze. "You promise?"

"I swear."

"Pinkie swear?"

"I don't know what that is," he replies, perplexed.

"Never mind, a regular swear is fine, I guess. Just don't mess this up."

Dad looks at me, but really he's looking beyond me, seeing something in his mind's eye. A memory maybe or something to come. Whatever it is, it haunts him. "In this situation," he says gravely, "messing up is simply not an option."

Three hours later I'm on a plane to San Francisco.

CHAPTER 2

NOW. SAN FRANCISCO. IN THE RAIN. YUP.

ONE OF DAD'S FAVORITE IDIOMS IS "CROSS THE stream where it is shallowest." This means the simple solution to a problem is usually the right one. Why go in the deep water and get soaked when you can walk across where the water comes up to your ankles? But if this were really *true*, I don't think I would be balanced precariously on a second-story window ledge outside a San Francisco mansion that looks like a wedding cake, in the dark, being pelted by cold winter rain.

How did I get here? Specifically, I came up the wall of climbing ivy to the window. Fortunately, security never considered a young criminal channeling her inner monkey or they would have gotten rid of the ivy first thing.

But *why* is the more important question. And to answer that, we have to go back to when I first arrived at Great-Aunt Irma's eight months ago. Everything was going fine. We were having fun. In fact, we were playing poker for pennies and I was *finally* winning, when we were interrupted by a man and a woman, in matching black suits and dark sunglasses despite the fact that it was night. Out of nowhere, they showed up at the door and everything went sideways.

Agent Star and Agent Fish claimed to be from an organization called Specialty Activities, a sub-sub-subdivision of the United States State Department. They were here to inform me that my father was dead. Great-Aunt Irma gasped at the news, clutching her purple sweater in disbelief while I examined the odd-couple agents. Their claim was *ridiculous*. I mean, come *on*. Much was wrong with this situation, starting with Star and Fish and ending with the absurd idea that Dad was dead.

"The globetrotting archaeologist?" I asked to clarify. "*That* Lawrence Benko?"

"Indeed." Agent Star's pants were too short and his socks didn't match. "It was a flash flood. A terrible scene. Chaos, mud, screaming. Two of Professor Benko's team members saw him washed away."

"We are sorry," said Agent Fish, who, come to think of it, kind of resembled a fish. But she didn't sound sorry. She sounded anxious, like she wanted to move on to the next thing on her list. Which she did. Very quickly. "Your father kept expedition notebooks, correct? Diaries of his findings? Notes?"

They had that part right, at least. Dad is never without a notebook. I half nodded in response.

"Do you have any idea the whereabouts of his latest notebook?" Fish asked urgently. "We understand he was looking for the magic Stone of Istenanya."

Really? In one breath they are telling me I'm an orphan and in the next they are asking after the Stone of Istenanya? It seemed inappropriate, all things considered. I told the agents that I did not have his notebook. And I reminded them the Stone of Istenanya is from a *fairy tale* my mother used to tell me before she left. Were they unaware that fairy tales are generally made up? More important, I informed them they were dead wrong about my dad being, well, *dead*. If some tragedy befell him, I'd *feel* it. And I didn't feel anything but hungry. Which meant something else happened.

But just try to tell the State Department they're wrong and see how far *you* get. Their tolerance for my many follow-up phone calls and pleading emails soon evaporated. It's *possible* I was banned from contacting them altogether. In fact, no one seemed interested in my theory that Dad was kidnapped or was suffering from amnesia. They patted me on the head condescendingly and told me time healed all wounds. It did not take long to realize that I had to take matters into my own hands and find him myself.

No big deal.

Of course, this was the exact moment my simple solution got very complicated. Several attempts to board an airplane to Budapest were, well, *unsuccessful*. And trying to get my hands on the information I knew Star and Fish were hiding didn't work out much better. The police were called. There were lectures about the definition of breaking and entering. And I might as well confess I got into some hot water borrowing my neighbor's self-driving car while investigating one of Dad's associates who was also supposed to be dead. Apparently, that is grand theft auto and frowned upon.

My plan to find my father wasn't working. I needed a new approach. And that's exactly when my art teacher happened to mention that in 1990 two men walked into Boston's Isabella Stewart Gardner Museum and left with five hundred million dollars' worth of paintings. It was the biggest art theft in history and they have never been caught! It occurred to me that a million dollars would go a long way to helping me find my father. I could buy plane and train tickets. I could pay bribes for information. The possibilities were endless! I just needed to get my hands on some valuable art. How hard could it be?

Which brings us back to the rain-slicked concrete ledge, where I cling like a drenched, B-team Spider-Man for dear life. From my precarious perch, I can just see my prize, a bronze sculpture of three ballerinas, recently purchased for one million bucks by Benedict Tewksbury, mysterious young tech mogul. No one has ever actually *seen* the guy, but that doesn't mean he's not a good person, donating heaps of money to charity, or so it said in the magazine article I found in Irma's pile of reading material.

And this makes me feel a little bit bad about taking his ballerinas, but it has turned out getting my hands on valuable art is not so simple. The article included a photo spread of Tewksbury's art collection, including one of his delightfully cute dog, Byte, sitting in front of the sculpture, which was perched on a pedestal.

But the photo also happened to capture a bit of the scenery *outside* the room's window, in particular a peculiar Monterey cypress tree that looked straight out of Dr.

Seuss, a tree I know well because I walk by it every day on my way to Holly Middle School. It was meant to be!

To be honest, a million dollars seems like a lot for three creepy, spindly ballerinas who wouldn't survive a minute of actual dancing, but I'm willing to overlook its dubious artistic value because further research showed the sculpture to be both backpack-size *and* unalarmed. Fabulous! This Tewksbury might be a genius, but he's not very smart.

The less-than-fabulous part, in addition to the rain and my slippery shoes, is sitting right there in a red velvet chair, wearing a baseball cap, barely visible in the shadows. *Why* is there a person in that chair? Is this actually Tewksbury *himself*? Am I the first person in the universe to see the real man? That's exciting and all, but mostly it's inconvenient. The billionaire genius is *not* supposed to be at home. I did two weeks of covert surveillance on my way to school and again on the return trip and there is never anyone in this house. Never. Ever.

Finally, after what feels like a geologic era, during which I have plenty of time to consider just how complicated my simple solution has become, the person inside rises slowly. There's lots of yawning and eye rubbing. This is good. It's late. Hey in there! You really should go to bed if you want to be awake enough tomorrow to add to your billions. Finally, Tewksbury shuffles out of the room, stopping just beyond the door to throw a glance back at the sculpture. Please hurry. I'm not sure how much longer I can hang on out here. As I gingerly shift my weight, the door closes and the genius is gone.

I'm on. I blow a wet strand of wayward hair from my eyes and pull out a special tool I designed, meant for jimmying windows from the outside. Necessity is the mother of invention, Dad always says, and the Window Witch 3.0 is absolutely necessary if I'm to get into this room.

The Window Witch 3.0 is flat metal on one end, so I can wiggle it under the closed window, and flexible enough to bend to whatever shape necessary. Once it's through, I squeeze the handle and a hook pops out that can liberate any window from its lock. I'm a little anxious on account of versions one and two involving law enforcement, but the window lock springs open with a satisfying pop and no alarms disturb the night. Clutching the wooden frame with one hand, I heave the window up with my shoulder.

Musty air blasts from the room, like wet dog, leftover meat loaf, and . . . moldy oranges? Yes, a sweet cloying smell, possibly from morning OJ spilled sometime last century and forgotten. Don't billionaires clean their houses? I throw my leg over the window ledge and wiggle inside. The carpet cushions my wet footsteps.

At long last I stand before my prize. The sculpture is even less impressive up close. I examine the pedestal to make sure it's not wired to an alarm system. Fortunately, my prize just sits there, as if the billionaire picked it up at a tag sale and not a Sotheby's art auction. My mouth is dry.

Gingerly I load the sculpture into my backpack. A few drops of water from my wet hair fall onto its shiny surface, but anything this expensive *must* be waterproof. Through the pack's thin nylon, a ballerina elbow stabs me in the spine. But there is no time to rearrange it now. I'll fix the problem as soon as I'm out of here and on solid ground.

I just need to get there. I slide through the open window, careful not to bump my precious cargo. Back out on the ledge, I pull the window shut behind me. The rain comes harder now and visibility is zero. Which means I'm not entirely sure how I lose my balance, slip off the ledge, and plunge two stories to the ground.

Does being dead hurt? Because I don't feel so good. I twist to find a large rosemary hedge holds me aloft. I wiggle and the hedge belches me to the ground. There's a sickening crack. Oh please, let it be my bones!

But it's not. It's the million-dollar ballerinas.

CHAPTER 3

CAUGHT

WHEN MY FATHER WENT MISSING, I ENDED UP IN the permanent care of Great-Aunt Irma, who favors brightly colored shirtdresses and Ugg boots no matter the season. She lives with Zeus in a drafty Victorian out in the avenues. The house is stuffed to the gills with creaky old furniture, science fiction paperbacks, magazines dated from before I was born, and random computer parts that no longer have any purpose other than to gather dust. There's a rope ladder in my room on the second floor in case the whole place goes up in flames and I have to make a quick escape.

Irma spends most of her day kicking back in an old recliner held together with duct tape. Laptop warming her thighs, she codes apps for senior citizens. Need to find your car in the parking lot? She's got you covered. Reminders to take your medication? Why, yes! Want to keep your brain sharp? Irma serves up regularly scheduled trivia questions and puzzles. She's created games that force you to socialize and even a dating app, which is by far her most popular.

"Why should us oldsters miss out on all the fun?" she asks. Great-Aunt Irma is on a first-name basis with a number of important CEOs and is often invited to speak at important conferences.

But she never goes. This is because she does not leave the house. Ever. For any reason. She says it's because Zeus cannot be alone, but the internet calls her condition "agoraphobia" and it's the reason she is not here in the emergency room with me as the doctor pokes and prods my body. I smell strongly of the rosemary hedge that cushioned my fall. Just serve me up with turkey, mashed potatoes, and cranberry sauce and call it Thanksgiving. For the record, everything hurts. My shoulder sports a big purple bruise and there's a bloody stab wound inches above my left butt check, compliments of the aggressively sharp elbows of those stupid ballerinas. When the doctor touches my swollen left wrist, I howl like a lost dog.

"We'll need an X-ray of that," she says, looping a

stethoscope around her neck. "Likely broken, but overall I'd say fortune smiled on you." Fortune? I don't think so. I'm left-handed. "This could have been serious." The doctor takes a step back just as Emily flies into the room. Uh-oh. There goes the peace and quiet.

"Lola!" Emily conveys relief, anger, and disappointment all with just my name. That takes talent. "Sorry, Doctor, I'm Emily Singleton, Lola's caseworker." That means she's the one in charge of making sure I stop ending up in the police station. This is not an easy job. "Is Lola okay?"

After assuring Emily that the bronze dancers got the worst of it, the doctor leaves to arrange for my X-ray. She must not notice the steam billowing from Emily's ears or she never would have left me here alone with her. It's not safe. I hang my head and try not to think about the trouble I'm in. Because from the look Emily's giving me, it's a lot.

Emily looms over me as I sit on the hospital bed, twirling a length of hair around my finger until the skin on my scalp sings. Usually Emily offers encouragement but not today.

"You could have died," she says flatly. "You fell two stories, not to mention the sculpture is a complete loss. The homeowner, a very influential community member, called the mayor and yelled at him about the high crime rates in this city. Do you think the mayor enjoyed being yelled at?" I'm smart enough to know this is a rhetorical question, one that doesn't require an answer. I stay very still. "And then the mayor called *me*. He wanted to know why delinquent kids are allowed to run wild in the streets. He said your rap sheet is longer than most of his speeches and we all know the mayor likes to talk. I can't make this one go away, Lola. You've gone too far. They are going to take action this time."

"Action" means I go up the river, check in at Club Fed, head to the slammer. I've been told it's a place out beyond the mountains, a campus of gray concrete buildings with bars on the windows and watery gruel at every meal. The inmates do hard labor all day, laundry and harvesting vegetables and making license plates. You're not allowed to laugh or have fun or read or play video games or anything. You're just a prisoner until you turn eighteen, after which they kick you out into a world that doesn't really want you back. My mouth goes dry. If I'm in lockdown, that means no one is looking for my father.

Emily scowls, pacing the small space like a caged animal. I feel a lecture coming on. I will get no sympathy, despite the stitches in my butt and my broken wrist. "You *promised* Great-Aunt Irma," Emily begins. Yep. A lecture. "And you promised me that you would behave. Why can't you apply this level of dedication to some other pursuit? Something legal perhaps? I cannot emphasize enough how disappointed I am."

Oh, I get it. Her disappointment practically glows. Emily's tried hard to unravel my propensity for crime. Her theory is that the loss of my father has driven me to indulge in risky, attention-seeking behavior. It's a nice theory. I like to encourage her so she doesn't feel bad about herself, but of course, she's totally wrong. At the moment, I'm in it for the cash.

"You promised you would go to school," she continues, waving her arms and practically taking out the blood pressure machine, "and do your homework and join the chess club and generally stay out of trouble. In case you were wondering, theft and intent to sell stolen property is *not* staying out of trouble. And you could have been seriously injured! Killed, even!"

For the record, I never committed to the chess club idea. At least not verbally. Strands of Emily's curly hair break free from her tight ponytail and form a frizzy halo around her head. She sits down hard beside me on the hospital bed. The paper crinkles.

"I know it's been rough," she says softly. "But you can't undo what's done, even if you hate it. You have to move on. We have to do better than this."

She is absolutely right. Something has to change.

I have to *stop* getting caught.

CHAPTER 4

WHAT COMES AFTER GETTING CAUGHT

I SIT ON A WOODEN BENCH OUTSIDE THE JUDGE'S office, my lime-green cast resting in my lap. The bench is tattooed with hearts bearing initials. It seems an odd place for a romantic declaration. And knives aren't allowed in here, so what would you carve with? A pencil? A really strong fingernail? While I'm pondering this, Emily comes to fetch me. Her expression is unreadable. I follow her into Judge Gold's office. It's not my first visit.

"Lola Benko," booms the judge as we stand before her. She's tall with white hair and a huge voice. She makes me nervous and not just because she holds my fate in her hands. "I'll be honest. I wish I weren't seeing you again so soon."

Judge Gold peers at my rap sheet through half-moon glasses. All those attempted plane rides, the breaking and entering, the self-driving car. She shakes the page at me. "Are you on a solo mission to wreck your life? What's next? The albino penguin at the zoo everyone is talking about?" Hold on. What's this about an albino penguin? "Don't you have friends you want to spend time with? Kids desperate to sign that cast?"

I shrug. The idea of real friends is nice, really nice even, but until recently, my nomadic lifestyle didn't make it practical. Who wants to be BFFs with a girl who is just going to up and leave? Besides, I don't have time to worry about friends. I need to stay focused on finding my father.

"I've seen your test scores," the judge says finally. "You're off the charts. You could do anything. Tell me why you do *this*."

Her words throw me back on my heels. We stare at each other. It's like she can see inside my brain, to the murky dark corners. Her eyes fill with something. Sadness? Recognition? Come on, Judge Gold! You're just supposed to ship me off to make license plates, not ask about my motivation.

Because the truth is, I don't know how to explain what *desperation* feels like. No one believes that my father is alive. No one will listen. "I don't know," I mumble in response.

"Of course you don't," the judge says, tossing aside my rap sheet. "You're twelve. Life is complicated. Now, listen closely. You've committed a serious crime. But even though it doesn't seem so, you are, right at this moment, very *lucky*. Strings have been pulled on your behalf. Your victim has decided not to press charges *if* you are willing to make some changes in your life."

I'm unclear on Judge Gold's definition of luck, but I know I don't have luck or strings. I keep my face neutral, unsure of what is going to happen next. Emily pats my head like I'm a baby chicken.

"Instead of being remanded to the juvenile detention facility in the mountains," the judge continues, "you will be sent to Redwood Academy, right here in San Francisco."

"The what?"

"Redwood Academy. It's a private school but, more important, a change of scene for you. A second chance."

"*Private* school?" My only experience with private schools is on television. Basically, beautiful people wearing expensive clothes and being mean to each other.

The judge offers me a sympathetic smile. "It's better than jail, wouldn't you agree?"

"Yes, ma'am," I say quickly, relief flooding my system. "Thank you, ma'am."

"Redwood is academically rigorous," the judge adds. "If all goes well, you will simply not have *time* to get into trouble. Win-win. And just so we're clear, this is the last chance this court will afford you."

"Thank you, Judge," says Emily. "I know Lola will try her absolute hardest to make this work."

I smile benignly, thinking about that albino penguin. Maybe it's time to go beyond art?

"Good luck, Lola," the judge says, dismissing me with a wave.

"Thank you, Judge," Emily repeats, grabbing my good wrist and pulling me from the judge's chambers. When we're clear of the building, she stops abruptly.

"This is great," she says, offering a grin. It looks weird, too big and wide. "A second chance. Or in your case a fifth or sixth chance, but who's counting?"

"What's Redwood Academy?" I ask quietly. Now, don't get me wrong. I'm no fan of Holly Middle School—it's boring and smells like bleach—but at least it's a known quantity.

"It was all Mr. Tewksbury's idea," Emily says. "He was uncomfortable with a kid being sent off to the detention center when the kid in question has had some tough times."

Now I feel extra guilty. I tried to take something from Tewksbury that didn't belong to me. Not only that, but I ruined it! And here he is, nicest man on the planet, giving me a second chance. For the moment, I've dodged a one-way trip to the gray buildings where I would spend the rest of my natural days laundering sheets and harvesting carrots.

Dad always says you make your own luck. But maybe, sometimes, luck happens anyway.

CHAPTER 5

REDWOOD ACADEMY, OR NOT PRISON

THE UNIFORM IS NOT LUCKY. IT'S A TERRIBLE horrible pleated skirt, scratchy knee socks, ugly brown loafers, and a button-down white shirt that will surely strangle me by day's end. I flush with anger as Great-Aunt Irma chortles in my bedroom doorway.

"You look *darling*," Irma says, her violet eyes gleeful. She pulls invisible lint off the uniform's matching red cardigan.

"Darling!" squawks Zeus, and I swear he rolls his glassy parrot eyes. That's it. Even the bird knows I look like a dork. I am *not* going outside like this. Judge Gold can send me to the slammer. I bet they have nicer uniforms.

"I look like a feral peacock." I groan. The best course of action would be to crawl back under my fluffy comforter, the one decorated with cute kittens and rainbows, and pretend to be invisible.

"You do not look like a feral peacock," Irma responds. After the crushed-ballerinas episode, I expected immediate grounding for life. Instead, Irma said that if the great Benedict Tewksbury could forgive me, then she could too. This was followed by a physics lesson on the nature of thin ice. It went on for quite a while and I understood that the consequences awaiting me if I screw up again will make kid prison up in the cold mountains look like a dream.

"This is a great opportunity," Irma continues. "I'd go back to seventh grade if I could."

She's obviously insane. No one wants to go *back* to seventh grade. I tug at the collar of the wretched shirt. I will not survive this day. I will die of humiliation before lunch.

Emily arrives in a cheery yellow Volkswagen Beetle to shepherd me to my first day at my new school. As we drive across town, she prattles on about how I'm going to love being challenged at Redwood. I barely listen as I click my newest tinkering project, a retractable thumb extension, in and out. Fastened from a spring, discarded scissors, and some wire, it's kind of like a modified whirligig but enables me to manipulate a pen and a fork while my hand is stuck in the annoying cast. I call it the ThumbBot 1.0. Of course, last night I shot applesauce all over the wall when I tried to use it with my spoon, but that's what version 2.0 is for. Dad says failure is just an invitation to improve. You have to try again and again. I shift in my seat, trying to keep the weight off my butt stitches. How am I going to sit through an entire day of classes? The kids are going to think I have fleas.

We head into the Presidio, a fifteen-hundred-acre park on the northern tip of San Francisco that used to be a military fort. It teems with eucalyptus trees, and soon Emily's cute yellow Beetle smells like day-old cat pee. These trees were brought here from Australia and their revenge is to stink up the place. We drive a few miles along a winding road, past old barracks rehabilitated to house a rock-climbing gym, a swim club, coffee shops, restaurants, and people, who apparently don't mind the smell. Groves of densely packed trees pass outside my window. I wonder if rats live in those trees. It seems like it would be a pleasant place to be a rat.

Lola! Stop it! Why are you thinking about rats? Stop thinking about rats right now!

I shake the image of happy rats hiding in clusters of trees from my head. No need to make a bad day worse. The entrance to Redwood is through two large stone pillars. Ominous, if you ask me, which no one does. The Beetle creeps along until a large building comes into view at the end of the driveway, surrounded by towering eucalyptus trees. The building is all sharp angles, glass and steel glinting in the pale February sun. Everything here is shiny and clean, photo-op ready. I can already tell this place is going to make Holly Middle School look like a dump.

"Nice, right?" Emily asks. I shrug. I'm still mad about the uniform. "Wait until you see the cafeteria. It has a view of the Golden Gate Bridge!" But does it have valuable art hanging on the walls, donated by rich alumni?

Emily reads my mind. "Don't even think about it," she says. I imagine that thin ice Irma was talking about. I can practically see through it to the icy water below. There might be fish down there. I have to be very careful.

"I was just thinking about how much I love the trees," I respond.

She gives me some serious side-eye. "You have a chance to turn it all around," she says. "The only thing that matters is what you do next." I'm smart enough to keep the snarky retort that bubbles up to myself.

Twenty minutes later, Emily is gone and I stand before the principal's big desk while she eyeballs me. Right away

I'm suspicious because she wears a pink woolly suit that looks like a sheep having a bad hair day and peers at me over bedazzled reading glasses.

"So," she says after a deliberate pause, "I'm Mrs. Boxley, principal of Redwood Academy, and you are Lola Benko, thief, correct?"

Oh, I don't like her already. Can I demand to be jailed? Would she wait patiently if I popped out to invent a principal-neutralizing ray gun? Probably not, but she does seem determined to wait for an answer, so I offer my best smile. "I didn't steal the sculpture," I say. "I tried, but instead I just ruined it."

Principal Boxley squeezes her lips into a tight line. "Is that so?"

"Yes. I don't want credit for something I didn't do."

"Wonderful." She grimaces, casting her eyes down to my file. "It says here that before Holly Middle School, you attended *ten* different schools in seven years?"

"Eleven," I clarify. "Probably the one in Ulaanbaatar isn't on there because we didn't really have, like, paper and stuff at that school. Or walls." When she gives me a funny look, I add that Ulaanbaatar is the capital of Mongolia.

"I *know* where Ulaanbaatar is," she responds sharply.

"Most people don't," I reply. "Because it's not really a tourist destination, if you know what I mean."

Principal Boxley squints at me, as if she can't really believe I'm here. "You certainly aren't shy," she says. I don't have much experience with regular school principals, but I'm pretty sure this is not a compliment. "We don't normally admit new students mid-term, especially those of questionable character. But an exception was made in your case as a *favor* to Mr. Tewksbury. He's a good man. A great man. A superlative human being in every way. Unlike, say, you."

Principal Boxley stands up and circles me. She wears high heels that click on the wood floor like angry crabs trying to scurry away. I stay as still as possible.

"We have a code of conduct here," she says. "High standards for behavior, integrity, and character. We tolerate no deviations."

"Yes, Mrs. Boxley."

"We are academically rigorous and disciplined. We strive and succeed. It's *my* reputation on the line whenever you kids screw up and I take my reputation very seriously. Do you understand?"

"Yes, Mrs. Boxley."

"Good."

Before she can torture me further, a boy comes charging into the room. He's a head taller than me, lanky with a shag of dark hair covering half his face. His uniform doesn't look nearly as dorky as mine. "Sorry—oh boy—I mean—sorry I'm late," he stammers. "There was a fire in the science lab and Liam hit Piper in the nose with the fire extinguisher by accident. And that was pretty bad. And then the sprinklers went off. It got a little out of hand."

Principal Boxley's expression darkens. "Well, that sounds like a problem," she says tersely. "Lola, this is Jin Wu-Rossi. He will be your guide today, to help get you oriented." She makes a little flicking motion with her wrist, dismissing us. I'm all too happy to comply. When we're a safe distance from the principal's office, Jin asks if I'm okay.

"Yeah," I say. "Why wouldn't I be?"

"Can't ever tell with the Jelly," he responds gravely.

"Who?"

"Mrs. Boxley, aka Box Jellyfish, aka the Jelly. She wraps you in her tentacles and it's instant death."

"She's that bad?"

"Worse."

"Great."

"We think she has self-esteem issues," Jin says, raising an eyebrow. "What happened to your wrist?"

I hold up my arm for a better view. "I fell two stories during a burglary," I say. "I crushed a million-dollar sculpture with my butt." I do not mention the stitches that itch something awful under the horrible wool skirt.

"You did not."

"I did."

The boy's dark eyes take me in, from the green cast and stiff uniform to the messy ponytail and ratty backpack. "What's with that thing on your thumb?"

"ThumbBot 1.0."

"Did you make it?"

I shift my weight from side to side. He's interrogating me. "Yes."

He narrows his gaze. "So you build things? Like, inventions?"

"I tinker. Yes." I'll say this, Jin is way better at interrogation than the many police officers it has been my pleasure (not really) to meet in the last eight months.

"Do you do this tinkering stuff a lot? I mean, are you good at it?"

Does he want to see my résumé? "Yes. I'm good at it."

"Would you call it STEM fair–level tinkering?"

I don't know what a STEM fair is, but if I admit this, I will *become* the dork I look like in this uniform and I don't want to be that person. I give a noncommittal nod while making a mental note to research STEM fairs later. I steel myself for another question, but Jin gets quiet, thinking.

"Lola Benko," he says finally. "You might be the most interesting thing to happen at Redwood since that eucalyptus tree fell over and crushed the medieval history section in the library last year."

Does he think this is a good thing or a bad thing?

I can't tell.

CHAPTER 6

EMOJABBER IS HOW WE ROLL.

IT MUST BE A GOOD THING BECAUSE JIN GRINS widely. "What's your EmoJabber handle?" he asks. "We can be friends. I mean, not real friends because I don't do real friends. Too much downside. But we can be fake friends. You know, social media *friends*. I'm in it for the numbers. I want to be massively virtually uber popular. So what is it?"

Who said anything about being friends, real or fake? I'm too busy for all of that. I have an albino penguin to liberate and a father to save. My priorities are set.

Jin very quickly determines my silence is cluelessness. "Do *not* tell me you don't have an EmoJabber handle.

Where have you been, under a rock?" In a way, yes. "Here, look at mine."

Jin pulls out a sleek black smartphone and starts tapping away while sneaking quick glances up and down the hallway. Finally, he shoves the phone at me. An app opens and the word "EmoJabber" appears, followed by a photo of Jin, under which are some symbols.

"It's texting entirely by emoji," he says excitedly, like he's letting me in on something big. Wait a minute. Slow down. Like, cave painting? But we have words. Hasn't anyone informed the EmoJabberers?

"It's a Tewksbury Tech thing," Jin continues.

Okay. Really. I know this mysterious Tewksbury character is awesome and everyone loves him and without him I'd be in jail, but does he *have* to be the center of every conversation?

"He's such a great guy he just gives it out for free. No ads. No spam. I'm on, like, three Tewksbury fan sites. He sponsors the citywide STEM fair every year. Did you know that? No? Jeez, there's a lot you don't know. Anyway, check it out. My EmoJabber handle is a sword, a doughnut, and a book. Because I like fencing."

"Fencing? People still do that?"

He scowls at me. That's probably one of those things that I should think but not say aloud, right? "The doughnut is obvious and the book because I like to read. Get it? It's only the best app ever. I wish I could meet him—Tewksbury, I mean. But he lets his work speak for itself."

"You mean no one has ever seen the guy, right? Isn't that a little, I don't know, strange?"

Jin appears to take my comment about Tewksbury as criticism. Quickly, he jumps to the Great One's defense. "Tewksbury is a genius. Geniuses are eccentric. Because they are geniuses. Get it?"

No. Not at all. But I know better than to say so. "Geniuses are eccentric," I repeat.

"Exactly. They are weird and odd and quirky and that's just fine because they are doing great things. And EmoJabber is *great*. Seriously. The most fun you will *ever* have. Here, give me your phone." He reaches out a hand.

This is *not* great. I do have one—a phone, that is. It's a hand-me-down from Irma and I'm 100 percent sure she installed a secret tracking app that sets off alarms if I get too close to an airport or the neighbor's car. Which is why the phone never leaves my desk. And I have no one to talk to anyway. But do I really want to tell Jin this? He already thinks I'm from the Dark Ages for not having an EmoJabber handle.

Fortunately, I'm saved from further humiliation by an

approaching teacher. "Mr. Wu-Rossi," the teacher booms. "You know the rules. Do I need to confiscate that phone?"

"No, sir! Sorry, sir!" Jin stuffs the phone back into his pocket.

The teacher looms over us. "Put it away in your locker."

"Absolutely. Right away. Yes, sir!" As the teacher continues down the hallway, Jin whispers, "No phones on campus. Last year, everyone was hunting monsters and it got seriously out of hand."

"Monsters?" I squeak.

"Monster Madness? Virtual reality game? You don't know that one either? Boy, you really *did* crawl out from under a rock! Anyway, who cares? Monster Madness is *so* last year. It's an emoji world now. Come on. I'll show you where the lockers are and we can pick up your schedule. Get ready. Redwood is hard-core."

As we walk, Jin describes what Redwood days are like. He speaks without pausing between words, swinging his long arms for emphasis. He tells me about his best friend, Paul. They were inseparable since kindergarten, but Paul moved away and now Jin's parents worry that he's lonely. He stops abruptly.

"But here's the thing. Even if I *am* lonely, is that worse than having a best-friend-size hole in my life? I mean, I need to figure out who I am and what I'm good at *without* Paul. And let me tell you, it's no fun." He starts walking again and I run to keep up. "Besides, I have other things to spend my time on. Important things. Like winning the STEM fair."

I nod like I totally know what he's talking about.

We continue with my orientation. Apparently, the French teacher hands out éclairs, the Spanish teacher hands out Fs, and the math teacher wears mismatched shoes but under no circumstances are you to mention it to her. Also, Mr. Kind, who teaches social studies, is very unkind, don't take classes with Ms. Perkins for any reason, don't be late for first period, and *never* eat the vanilla pudding in the cafeteria. It gives you gas. Uniformed students rush past as I struggle along in Jin's wake of information. My head spins.

"Don't worry," Jin says finally. "Soon you'll be 'academized' and you won't feel any pain. It's kind of like a lobotomy but way worse." So that's it. I'm to be a zombie in an awful outfit. Generally, I try not to be mad at my father for disappearing and leaving me here in this weird middle-school universe, but right now I could probably spare a few minutes.

We leave the main building, which is classrooms, offices,

and lockers, and cross an outside quad, filled with a bunch of tables and chairs. Leading from the quad is a series of paved walkways to other Redwood buildings, including the library, the cafeteria, and the gymnasium. In the middle of the quad is a large fountain. Poseidon spits water out of his mouth all over a bunch of concrete dolphins, in a very undignified way. Students sit in tight clusters. Laughter and shouting fill the air, and all at once I experience the familiar prickling sensation of being an outsider.

Occasionally, living out of my suitcase, I longed for the ordinary—bedroom walls covered in cute puppy posters, bookshelves, a spot on a soccer team with red uniforms, a cat named Fluffy who slept on my feet, a birthday cake with thick icing flowers and actual candles, that real friend I couldn't quite manage, an *address*. I craved a sense of belonging.

Dad never suspected and I didn't want to hurt his feelings by complaining, but sometimes I still dreamed about real friends and birthday cakes anyway.

CHAPTER 7

THE AMAZING TERRAIN INSIDE GREAT-AUNT IRMA'S HEAD

I DON'T KNOW IF I'M "ACADEMIZED" YET, BUT I SURE am tired. I got lost six times at school. I swear someone kept moving my locker. Finding the bathroom gave me fits. My skirt gave me a rash. ThumbBot 1.0 exploded in the cafeteria, springs and scissor parts flying everywhere, which was seven different kinds of embarrassing. And the unkind Mr. Kind made me recite the first two articles of the Bill of Rights because I was twenty-seven seconds late to class.

In addition to math, science, English, and social studies, we did yoga, ran laps, mastered an obstacle course that felt a little Beast Master to me, and played a speed round of dodgeball to the death. I also test-drove the enormous Redwood library by doing a deep dive into albino penguins. Did you know they are very rare and worth a fortune? By the time I drag through the front door of the old Victorian, I'm barely upright. My wrist aches in the sweaty cast. My butt stitches itch.

"Stick a fork in me," I shout, tossing my ten-ton backpack on the floor. "I'm done!"

Zeus greets me with a hideously loud "Welcome, darling!" but Irma does not. She's too busy lurching around the kitchen, arms extended like the little old lady version of Frankenstein's monster. Her dress is safety orange, her furry boots dark brown. Virtual reality headsets are usually bulky, but not Irma's. Her goggles, sleek and lightweight, wear like a pair of sporty silver sunglasses, most likely given to her by a fancy tech company to trial and report back.

"Lola, is that you?" she says, stumbling into the kitchen table. "Ouch! I'm about to fly over the Grand Canyon. These goggles rock. Hold on. Here I go." She throws her arms out like wings and for a moment I think she might fall flat on her face, but instead she lets loose a scream, equal parts terror and exhilaration.

"I'm a bird!" she yells. "These are the best! That Tewksbury is a genius!"

Tewksbury the mysterious genius *again*? That reminds me I need to investigate these STEM fairs he sponsors so I do not appear so clueless to my new classmates. As Irma soars around the room, bumping into furniture and appliances, Zeus looks on with disgust and I retreat into the hallway for personal safety. New technology gets her worked up, like she just downed ten espresso shots.

As Irma hoots and hollers about the majesty of the Grand Canyon, the house phone erupts in the background. Zeus immediately goes bananas, mimicking the ring until I can't stand it anymore. I grab the handset and dash into the backyard for quiet. "Hello?"

"Is this Irma Benko?" a bored voice inquires.

I'm about to say that Irma is busy flying like an eagle over the Grand Canyon but decide it is much less complicated to lie. "Yes."

"Great. This is Roger at Bay Area Mini Storage. Wait, do I hear a bird?"

"No," I say flatly.

"Really? I swear I—"

"No birds," I interrupt.

"Wow. Okay, then. The reason I'm calling is to ask if you have received our mailed past-due notices?"

"Um, no?"

The man sighs extravagantly. It takes forever, like a balloon with a slow leak. "Well, you're four months behind on payments for your storage unit." Wait. Irma has *more* stuff? How is that even possible? I envision forgotten furniture, moldy carpets, malfunctioning light fixtures, and dusty books. I'm just about to tell the guy that Irma will call him back when it occurs to me that a neglected storage unit might also contain valuable items, items that would not be *missed*. And these items would certainly be easier to acquire than an albino penguin.

"That's terrible," I say with mock sincerity. "My assistant must have messed up. I will get on this right away. What did you say your address was again? And the unit number?"

Of course, I want to run right down to the Marina and break in to unit number seventeen, but I'm keenly aware that this is my last chance at pretending to go straight. Judge Gold's personal reputation is on the line, and if I screw up, she will make sure I'm never heard from again. I have to proceed with the utmost caution, which means playing along. And playing along means math homework, specifically seven questions dealing with spatial sense and data analysis. And a personal essay about a historical figure of interest. And phases of the moon research for science.

During dinner, Irma quizzes me on school. She wants

details on the kids, the campus, the teachers, the principal. Who did I talk to? Did I make friends? I'm forced to
describe my turkey sandwich right down to the brand of
mustard smeared on the sourdough bread. She seems satisfied when I say Dijon, a little on the spicy side. It's as if
she wants proof that I was *actually* there and not off stealing a Monet or that cute little albino penguin. There is no
denying my credibility is at an all-time low.

I have to be careful.

CHAPTER 8

PANCAKES WITH A SIDE OF HANNAH HILL

IT'S MY FIRST REAL DAY AT REDWOOD, BUT ALL I can think about are storage lockers full of forgotten treasure. Gold bricks, first-edition Mark Twains, two-pound emeralds. Okay, maybe a two-pound gem is unreasonable, but there could be *smaller* pieces of jewelry, diamond earrings or ruby bracelets or something, from back in the day when Irma used to go out of the house. No matter what, for the first time since falling on the ballerinas, I'm excited by the possibilities. I'm back on track. Mission is a go. Hang in there, Dad, I'm coming!

Jin waits for me, pacing in front of the lockers. He flips

his long hair out of his eyes every fifteen seconds. How does a person live like that?

"Where have you *been*?" he demands as I try to remember my locker combination. I know there's a four in there somewhere. Maybe a seven? Hair flip.

"What do you mean?" I ask. "It's not even seven thirty yet." And today there was no Emily express. I'm back to public transportation, which means I rolled out the door at six thirty in the morning. It was dark. There were stars. I yawn for emphasis.

"I know, but you should get here in time for breakfast," Jin says. "The pancakes are killer, worth the price of tuition alone." Another hair flip.

"Do you want a hair elastic?" I ask.

"Huh?"

"Never mind."

"Anyway, I need to *tell* you something."

"What?" I ask. Maybe it's a six in the combination and not a four? How badly do I really need what is in this locker anyway?

Jin furrows his brow. "Can I trust you?" Hair flip.

"Sure." Nope. Not six.

"Swear?"

"That you can trust me?" I ask, giving up on my locker.

His gaze indicates he's quite serious. But we're not even friends! Jin doesn't do friends, so what's this about? "Okay. Fine. I *swear* on Zeus that you can trust me."

"The Greek god?"

"No. The bird. Now spill it."

But instead of conspiratorial whispering, Jin motions for me to follow. We end up outside on the quad. Fog lingers and a steady cold breeze blows, but the space is crowded with students shoveling killer pancakes into their mouths before the bell rings. My stomach rumbles. Jin takes an empty table and indicates I should sit.

"Don't be obvious, but check out my *nemesis*," he growls, pointing with his elbow in a way I think he thinks is subtle. "Hannah Hill."

Hannah Hill sits at a table, nose in a book, pancakes neglected. The elbows of her uniform sweater are worn. Her dark red hair hangs down well past her shoulders. All around her, tables overflow with kids, but the seats at her table are vacant. To be honest, she doesn't look like nemesis material. She looks very alone. "What did she do to you?"

"What did she do? What did she *do*? Where do I even begin?"

"At the beginning?" I suggest.

Jin fixes me in an intense gaze. "Well, to start with, she is a fun-sucking vortex. She *never* laughs."

"Maybe she doesn't think you're funny?"

"Quit interrupting. Okay, occasionally she cackles like the Wicked Witch of the West, but that doesn't count. And she always does the extra credit in math, completely killing the grading curve. Every. Single. Time."

"You don't like her because she's smart and works hard?"

"No! That's not it at all."

Clearly, I'm missing something. "You'd better explain."

Jin sighs, exasperated. "We're tied for the most STEM fair wins ever, in the history of the world of STEM fairs. *Three* each." Ah, now I see. She's the competition. "And listen carefully because this part is important. This year the STEM fair grand prize is a trip to NASA summer camp. You get to drive the Mars rover!"

"No way they'd let a kid drive the rover," I protest.

"They will if you win the STEM fair. It's only like the most important thing that happens in San Francisco, maybe even the country. And I plan to win. It won't be easy and Hannah will do *anything* to beat the competition, even play dirty. Last year, she 'accidentally' tripped and spilled an entire blueberry smoothie all over Simon's perpetual motion machine. Let me tell you. That was no accident." I can see how this would be irritating. A spilled smoothie is a real mess.

Like a ghost, Hannah materializes at our table. Jin locks eyes with her. In the Wild West, this is the part where someone would yell "Draw!"

"Lola," Jin says through gritted teeth. "Did I mention that during the class trip to the zoo Hannah got motion sick and barfed all over the bus? Can you imagine the mess if they took her up in a NASA vomit comet and she puked in her spacesuit?" Jin snorts with laughter.

"You sound like a dork when you do that," Hannah says. "Like a goose being strangled." She looms over us. Despite the chill, I sweat a little under the collar of my shirt. She gives off a serious vibe, like she is not messing around. "And for the record, it's *not* a vomit comet. It's an antigravity plane and seasoned astronauts throw up in it all the time. But you'll never find out, because you don't have a prayer of winning the competition without Paul. He was the brains of your operation. Everyone knows *that*."

Jin's nostrils flare. "At least I *had* a teammate."

Uh-oh. This is getting ugly. Hannah's cheeks burn. "I *choose* to work alone," she snaps. "I don't have time for the complications of other *people*."

"That's a good one. Really, no one wants to hang out

with you because you won't even let your teammates go home for dinner or do their homework or go to the bathroom."

"Success requires sacrifice," Hannah hisses. "Not that you would know anything about that." My adrenaline surges as I prepare to launch myself between them before they come to blows.

"You have no idea what you're talking about," Jin says, his voice shrill. "Paul and I shared the work. We were equal partners. He didn't *own* me."

I'd say in terms of insulting each other, they are also tied. I wait to see what is going to happen next. Will someone throw pancakes? Will there be pandemonium?

Hannah offers a condescending smile. "You keep on telling yourself that." Jin's hands ball into tight fists. I'm busy watching the back-and-forth and therefore completely unprepared when her attention turns to me.

"You must be Lola the art thief," she says.

"Failed art thief," I mumble.

"Who cares? I'm impressed. I also heard you've partnered with Jin for the STEM fair. You must be brave, too. Or stupid. I don't know which."

My head pivots toward Jin, whose eyes plead with me not to bust him. "Sure," I say after a pause.

Hannah's eyebrow spikes. "And, New Paul, I hear you're building an electromagnetic pulse generator?"

"We are?" Is *this* his plan to get back on the winners' podium? I have some thoughts to share on that.

"How . . . interesting." She studies me. I squirm. "Well, don't say I didn't warn you, Lola the art thief."

"*Failed* art thief," I repeat. As soon as she is out of earshot, I turn to a sheepish Jin.

"*Partners? New Paul?*"

"I am *so* sorry, but she was up in my business about how I can't cut it without Paul and I just snapped and threw your name out there and then I couldn't take it back."

"An *electromagnetic pulse generator*?"

"I thought it would be cool. You know, mess up everyone's electronics. But don't worry. I've made a lot of progress on the project. It'll be easy! You'll barely have to do anything!" His eyes search my face for some indication of how this is going to end up.

But think about it. If I'm involved in a STEM fair project, Irma and Emily *cannot* be suspicious of my behavior. STEM fair projects have "playing along" written all over them. They can also provide cover when necessary.

"Fine," I say. "I'll do it."

Jin grins. "Paul used to say I trusted too much in

feelings and that was bad, but the minute I saw the ThumbBot, I knew we were destined to be partners. You are *exactly* what this project needs."

After school, I take a detour to the Marina to case Bay Area Mini Storage and I have a feeling too. A bad one. There are security cameras everywhere and a chain-link fence topped with coils of razor wire. There's a gate secured with an electronic keypad requiring an entrance code. There might be an angry dog. I sit on a bench across the street and scowl. Bay Area Mini Storage is definitely a two-handed job and I'm one hand short, stuck in the smelly green cast for four more weeks. I pull a purloined apple from my overstuffed backpack and take a bite. There has to be a solution to this problem.

How about a mechanical hand? Irma has one of those garbage grabbers she uses to pull stuff off high shelves. Maybe with some wire, glue, and oven mitts I could reconfigure it into something to get me over that fence. I'd call it Mittens 1.0. It might work.

Unless it's raining. And the glue melts. And the wire rusts. And the grabber snaps in two. And I get hung up on a bunch of razor wire. Which leaves me *caught*.

As I sit there, contemplating the future failure of the nonexistent Mittens, another idea forms in my head. It's not a good idea either. It's a terrible idea. Why would I even *entertain* such an idea? There is no good reason to ask a perfect stranger for help. Okay, I guess Jin is not a perfect stranger—we are STEM fair teammates, after all—but I just met him and we are definitely not friends. He'd probably call the police or tell his parents or, worse, confess to Principal Boxley.

Forget it. As I pitch my apple core into a trash bin, I vow to find another way into the storage locker.

CHAPTER 9

LOLA BENKO, BIG MOUTH

THE NEXT AFTERNOON, AFTER BARELY SURVIVING A friendly game of Capture the Flag on Redwood's expansive lawn, but having much better luck opening my locker, my plan is to return to Bay Area Mini Storage and devise a one-handed strategy to get inside unit seventeen that doesn't earn me a return visit to Judge Gold's courtroom. Dad always says don't be afraid to go back to square one. But Jin waits at the lockers, flicking his hair around more than usual, and I sense my plan is headed for derailment.

"If we are going to win gold in the STEM fair," he says sternly, "we have to get started *right* away. I'm sure

Hannah has already built a tinfoil satellite to detect alien life on Pluto or something by now." He rolls his eyes. I feel some pressure, having only just learned what a STEM fair *is*. And who said anything about *gold*? I have been misled.

"You can come to my house," Jin continues, stuffing random books into my backpack and hurling it at me. "Let's go." Clearly no is not an answer Jin is willing to accept. I dutifully follow him out the Redwood gates and down the sidewalk to the closest bus stop. My Bay Area Mini Storage break-in breakthrough will have to wait.

Jin lives out in a nice neighborhood with steep hills and a high percentage of sunny days for San Francisco. His house is a Painted Lady Victorian, pink and purple with gold trim. It glows with warmth, and as soon as the orange front door springs open, I'm hit with the most delicious smells. Sweet fragrant spices permeate the air.

"Mom? Dad?" Jin yells, kicking off his shoes and dumping his jacket on the ground. "I'm home." Out of nowhere, a blur barrels down the hallway and hits Jin full-on. He tumbles backward with a grunt. "Get off me!"

Pinning Jin to the ground is a small person in a Batman hoodie. "Lola, meet my little brother, Bart, aka fart face."

Jin's mother appears. She has a beautiful smile and

long dark hair twisted into a bun impaled by two pencils. "Boys, enough. Who's your friend?"

"This is Lola," Jin says, shoving his brother aside. "We are STEM fair partners. We are *not* friends. Remember I told you I'm not doing that anymore?"

His mother sighs. "Right. Silly me. Well, welcome, Lola, STEM fair partner. I'm Julia."

"Boo-hoo," Bart yells, dancing wildly around. "Paul moved to New York."

"Shut. Up."

"It smells so good in here," I remark.

"Oh, that's just the casserole thingy," says Jin.

Julia offers a conspiratorial smile. "It's something Jin's dad, Marco, invented and it's really quite good, even if none of us can remember what it's called. Would you like to join us for dinner?"

"*Mom.*"

"I can't allow you to starve your STEM fair partner," Julia says firmly. "Besides, your dad makes enough food to feed an army. Lola would be doing us a favor. Will you stay?"

Beside me, Jin glowers. But the house smells so good and it's been months since I've eaten anything but takeout, so I blurt out yes before I can stop myself.

"Great," Julia says with a wide grin much like Jin's. "Make sure to let your parents know."

"I live with my aunt. Actually, my great-aunt. Irma."

Julia's eyes drift to my cast. "Well, give her a call so she doesn't worry. Forty-five minutes until dinner. Now go get to work on that project."

"We'll be in the lab!" Jin yells, racing down the hallway as I scurry to keep up. "No fart faces allowed!" Bart watches us go with sad eyes. His lower lip trembles. I stumble after Jin, through the kitchen, where his father is wearing eye protection and an apron. He's tall with a slight stoop to his shoulders, dark hair shot through with gray.

"Jin!" he bellows in accented English as we screech to a stop on the faded kitchen tile. "Have a taste." He holds out a wooden spoon with a bit of something that looks like pasta sauce. "I'm not sure if the seasoning is right. This casserole thingy can be tricky."

Jin dutifully steps forward and slurps up the offering. He tilts his head to one side, brows furrowed. "More cayenne, more salt, a pinch of sugar, and a cinnamon stick," he pronounces.

All that from a single spoonful? Does he have magic taste buds? Marco palm-slaps his own forehead. "Of course! Cinnamon. Jin the genius." He gives Jin a big kiss on the top of his head and Jin looks ready to keel over dead from embarrassment.

"Dad!"

"Sorry, sorry. Go about your business. Oh wait, who are you?" Marco has just now noticed me standing in his kitchen. "Are you a new friend of Jin's?"

Oh boy, here we go again. Marco yanks off one of his oven mitts and offers me his hand. We shake vigorously. I might lose the use of my right arm, and I'm already down the left.

"This is Lola," Jin mumbles. "We're working on the STEM fair project. That is *all*."

"Excellent," Marco says. "Are you staying for the casserole thingy?"

"Yes," Jin says, annoyed. "Can we go now?"

Marco waves us off. "Go and be brilliant while I whip up greatness in the kitchen."

We bolt out the door leading to the backyard. Across the tiny patch of lawn, against the fence, is a stand-alone studio that must be the lab. When Jin flicks on the lights, I gasp. It's a true maker space, a hacker's lab on steroids. There's a 3D printer, a laser cutter, a CNC machine, a 3D scanner, a welder, an actual soldering station, and an oscilloscope. And that's just what I can see from the door. I might be drooling.

"Cool, right?"

"That is so not the right word," I reply. At Irma's, I make do with a small box of tools, duct tape, scissors, string, superglue, some other junk. But this is another league entirely.

"It's all my mom," Jin explains. "She likes to make stuff. She made this mad robot once that was supposed to clean our windows, but instead it just went full-on banshee and smashed them all. Hi-larious."

That's it. I'm moving in. "I like your parents," I say.

"They're okay, I guess," he responds, grimacing. "They met at the Uffizi in Florence."

"The museum?" Boy, one piece of art from their collection and I'd be *set*.

"Yeah. My dad is Italian and my mom was on a semester abroad in Florence. They were both admiring a Botticelli—you know that artist who likes big hair—when they noticed each other and fell instantly in love. Gross."

I smile, at once warm and uncomfortable. I have no idea how my parents met. Jin has chapters in his story that I don't. "Not gross," I say.

"Anyway," Jin continues, "my mom wanted to come

back to her family in San Francisco and my dad couldn't stand to be away from her and now I'm saddled with the weirdest hyphenated last name *ever*. So how did *you* end up at Redwood?"

"A judge sent me. Instead of jail."

Jin snorts. "Is there a difference?"

"Yes." I get down on my knees for a better view of the 3D printer. Stacked next to it are spools of the colorful filament used to print objects. Imagine the ThumbBot 2.0 if I had access to this! "In jail," I say, "I can't look for my father."

There's an awkward silence. Jin focuses on a space just over my left shoulder. "Um. Well. I heard your father was . . . had passed away."

"No way." My cheeks flush. "But no one seems to want to find him but me."

Jin drums his fingers on the table, brows creased. "You'd better back up and tell me the whole story because right now I'm totally confused."

I fiddle with the end of the purple filament, surprised at how strong the urge is to do just that, tell him everything. I give myself a mental kick in the shins. I'm supposed to be reformed. I'm supposed to have accepted my father's death and moved on. And I don't know Jin at *all*.

What if he tells the Jelly and she tells Emily and she tells Judge Gold and I end up in the slammer anyway? Who rescues Dad then? But before I can stop myself, the story bubbles up and spills out, like so much milk from an overturned carton.

CHAPTER 10

FRANKENSTEIN 1.0, OR WHERE IS THAT FIRE EXTINGUISHER AGAIN?

WHEN I FINISH, JIN STARES AT ME, EYES BRIGHT and agitated. "You stole a *car*?"

"Borrowed. I fully intended to return it."

He waves off this explanation. "Whatever. Paul always tells me my ideas are stupid. Boy, he'd be super impressed with you. And you were really going to sell the ballerinas on the black market?"

"Well, I couldn't exactly put it up on eBay, could I?"

Jin shakes his head, in disbelief or amazement. I can't tell which. "All to use the proceeds to bribe people for information about your dad."

"And for travel expenses."

"Do you even know where to start looking or are you just planning on wandering around Europe until you find him?"

Put that way, my plan sounds a little stupid. "That's not it exactly—" I begin.

But Jin interrupts. "And even though you promised the judge you'd behave, you sound like you have no intention of stopping."

"I need to find my father. If you have any suggestions on how I might do it better, I'd love to hear them."

"Hold on." Jin jumps from his stool and starts pawing through the surrounding cabinets, eventually pulling out a plastic bin and plunking it on the table between us. I peer into the bin at a sad mess of metal parts and bits of plastic.

"Do not tell me this is *it*," I say flatly.

He gives a twitchy smile and fixes me in an intense gaze. "Now, I'm not known for having good ideas, but what if you help me win the STEM fair and I help you find your father?"

Huh? I never *asked* for help. But Jin cuts me off before I can tell him so.

"Just hear me out," he says, gesturing to the bin of parts. "Obviously, what I told you before about being mostly done is not exactly true. I admit it. I need help. But it sounds like you need help too. You haven't found your dad yet."

"And what do *you* know about finding missing people?" I ask.

"Nothing," he says bluntly. "But two brains are better than one. We have twice the chance of winning the STEM fair and twice the possibility of finding your dad. It's just math."

He's right, even if I don't want to admit it. Finding my father has so far been a complete failure. Maybe extra brainpower is the answer because my single brain sure isn't getting the job done. I pull the bin closer and take another look.

"Are baking soda volcanoes out of the question?" I ask.

"Is that a yes?"

I shrug. "I guess." I already spilled all my secrets. How much worse can Jin's assistance make my already bad situation? Who knows, maybe he will even come up with a good idea.

Jin's eyes flood with relief. "This is so great. And volcanoes are for kindergartners. We need our pulse to *work*."

"Don't panic." True, our project is seriously ill, but at least this is a problem I have a chance of fixing. We pull a couple of stools around the table, and Jin turns on bright overhead lights, which serve only to make the project look worse. Hunks of plastic and wire are everywhere. It's bad. I force a smile. "We'll figure it out."

"You think so?" Jin beams, thrilling to a rescue I have yet to perform.

But how hard can it be to invent an electromagnetic pulse electricity disruptor device that a) doesn't get us arrested for possessing weapons of mass destruction, and b) wins a super-competitive STEM fair? But I distinctly remember thinking being an art thief would be easy too, and look what happened there. I shake off the feeling. In these situations, sometimes it's better not to dwell on the specifics. They will only stress you out.

"We have to start at the beginning," I say confidently, scooping up a circuit from the table and examining it.

Jin nods. "Just tell me what to do."

Heads down, we get to work. Of course, saving us from STEM fair humiliation is more challenging with a broken wrist. I end up barking a lot of orders at Jin, who good-naturedly executes them without complaint.

Finally, Julia calls us in for dinner. The casserole thingy is delicious and I have three helpings. Marco serves us homemade soda, made by pouring sweet Italian syrup into sparkling water.

Jin rolls his eyes. "No real soda."

"I make the syrups myself," Marco reports, obviously proud. "That way we can experiment with flavors. Ginger, thyme, rose petal, basil."

"Dog poop," Bart suggests, earning a side-eye from his mother.

While we eat, Jin's parents quiz us about our day. They want details. Bart is clearly miserable during this recitation of events that have nothing to do with him and covertly flings peas at the far wall with his spoon. His aim is good. He's got them bouncing off the refrigerator and landing in the sink. After dinner, Julia serves us bowls of ice cream drenched in butterscotch sauce.

"Take them back to the lab if you want," she says. So here I sit in a warm space full of cool stuff, eating a cold treat. I might be inadvertently *enjoying* myself. It's awfully distracting.

"How'd you learn to do all this stuff?" Jin asks as I feebly attempt to weld two circuits together.

"Necessity is the mother of invention," I say.

"Did you make that up?"

"It's something my dad says. If you need a technology that doesn't exist yet, you just have to make it. Like when scientists wanted to explore the Mariana Trench or outer space, they had to invent a way to get there. Or maybe you need to open a hidden tomb without messing it up. Or, say, get in through a locked window from the outside."

"Paul was good at this stuff," Jin says thoughtfully. "But you might be better."

My cheeks flush. "Thanks. But we have a problem. Power. We need more. Some kind of bigger, better battery."

Jin groans. "Yes! Why didn't I think of that?" He digs frantically through a cabinet, ignoring his ice cream. To be polite, I eat it before it melts.

Finally, he emerges, holding up something that looks like an octopus ate an old car battery. Dropping it on the table with a thud, Jin grins, like he knows a secret. "My mom was trying to boost the power for Bart's RC Roadster. But this thing melted the whole car!" He seems pleased by the catastrophic failure that befell his little brother's beloved roadster. "It was *totally* overpowered. But it might work for the pulse."

"We can modify it," I say.

We set to work, not talking much. When we're done, the pulse device is about the length of a shoebox and looks like a plastic rolling pin on life support propped up against the battery octopus. Wires poke out everywhere. Inside the rolling pin is a small glowing crystal, made of glass, given to Jin's mother by his father on some anniversary and subsequently repurposed by Jin. I attach the last wires, purple and yellow.

"It's ugly." Jin frowns.

"Function over form," I say.

"Isn't that what they said about Frankenstein's monster? Wait a sec." He pulls open a drawer in one of the cabinets and produces a set of googly eyes and a handful of turquoise pipe cleaners. He sticks the eyes onto Frank 1.0's plastic exoskeleton and, after fashioning rabbit ears from the pipe cleaners, adds those, too. Frank now resembles a demented bunny. Is this an improvement? Jin seems to think so. "Cool."

"Let's test him."

Jin hands me a pair of safety glasses. "Better put these on. No telling what's going to happen." My heart thumps against my ribs. I connected the wires in the right sequence, didn't I? I double-checked? Well, it's too late now. Jin flips the switch to activate our STEM fair project.

What happens next is very exciting and I don't mean in a good way. The rolling pin begins to vibrate faster and faster. The crystal glows red-hot, melting the googly eyes while the surrounding plastic bubbles up. Sparks fly off the battery as the wires attached to the leads sizzle and spit. The bunny ears instantly fry.

"Turn it off!" I yell. Jin flails at the switch but leaps back. It's scorching. The melting plastic of the rolling pin begins to expand, like a balloon. "It's gonna blow!" The wires erupt into tiny fireworks. Using my cast, I shove the device away from us and grab a fire extinguisher from the corner of the lab. The entire canister is covered with instructions for use, but I don't have time for that. Our pulse device is set to explode and we're going to need more than safety glasses to survive unscathed. I detach the nozzle, aim, and press all the levers and buttons. A spray of white foam gushes forth and smothers the device. It crackles and pops. It's only then I realize Jin is hiding behind me with his eyes closed.

"Is it over?" he whispers.

"Yes," I say. "Too much power."

Footsteps in the yard draw our attention. "My dad!" We grab a big metal bin and shovel the smoldering remains of the project inside, jamming on the lid. But there's still smoke.

"Your cast!" I glance down to see tendrils of smoke rising from my singed cast, dark with soot. Jin dumps the rest of his fake soda over it and it smolders like doused firewood. I tuck it behind my back just as Marco strides through the door. He stops abruptly.

"It smells funny in here." His forehead crinkles with concern. With my foot, I edge the fire extinguisher out of sight.

"We spilled some stuff," I say quickly. "It's mostly cleaned up now."

"Well, you know what they say," Marco replies with a wink. "Fail often, fail fast. Just don't burn down the house." He laughs as he scoops up our empty ice cream bowls. I grin, hoping he doesn't notice the puff of smoke rising behind my back. When Marco finally leaves, we burst out laughing, hee-hawing like a couple of insane donkeys.

"It's still smoking," Jin says, tears streaming down his cheeks. "And your cast! It's falling apart!"

"Is 'Fail often, fail fast, don't burn down the house' something *your* dad always says?" I ask.

Jin can barely answer, doubled over with laughter. "It is! Oh man, right now I am *so* happy that you screwed up your robbery and got banished to Redwood. We make a great team."

Despite my possibly singed eyebrows, I feel lighter somehow. *I* know we are not real friends, but my smile sure doesn't.

CHAPTER 11

MY RIGHT-HAND MAN

GREAT-AUNT IRMA MISTAKENLY ASSUMES I'VE MADE a friend and is positively thrilled. "I am positively thrilled," she says when I get home. "But why do you smell like burnt plastic? And *what* happened to your cast?"

Explaining that Frank 1.0 blew up seems a bad way to keep a low profile, so I concoct a story about Jin and me building a baking soda volcano and the magma getting all over my cast. Parts of my story are true, anyway.

"I should have paid more attention to what we were doing," I say. "And not ruined my cast."

But Irma doesn't care about the cast. She's so happy about the new friend part that I don't have the heart to tell her it's more of a business arrangement. I help Jin. Jin helps me. Eventually, I slink away to my room under the guise of having tons of homework. From my backpack, I pull out the still-smoldering remains of Frank 1.0 and plunk him down on my desk. His remaining bunny ear turns to cinder in my hands. I have work to do to make Frank 2.0 a reality. He'll need a sleeker design and a more reliable battery, and I'll have to get control of the wiring. No big deal. I begin to sketch out my initial ideas on a piece of notebook paper. I'm so lost in planning that when my phone squawks for attention, I jump. I actually gave Jin my number because that seemed like a normal thing to do, so I have no business being surprised he's using it.

Jin: You need to set up EmoJabber! It's so much more fun than regular text! I have a handle for you and everything. 📖
🧑‍🦰🪄 *What do you think? Do you like it?*

I stare at the emojis. The book part is okay, I guess, although I'm a little offended by the stick of dynamite.

Jin: Well?

Me: It's great. Shouldn't Jin be elbow-deep in his math set or something? Shouldn't I be too?

Jin: So how do we get into this storage locker? And is it definitely easier than the albino penguin?

Seriously. Did I have to tell him about the penguin?

Me: Storage locker definitely easier than penguin. But I haven't figured out how to get in yet.

Jin: Take two minutes and brainstorm. Report back.

Who *is* this kid? I go back to tinkering with Frank but don't make much progress before Jin texts me again.

Jin: My ideas aren't great, but I have one.

Me: Can you stop saying that?

Jin: What?

Me: About your ideas being bad. How do you know?

Jin: Believe me. I know. Paul told me all the time.

I have a problem with this Paul person and I don't even know him. Aren't best friends supposed to make you feel good about yourself? Paul sure wasn't doing much for Jin's confidence.

Me: Who cares what Paul thinks? He's not here.

There's a pause during which I can't tell if I have offended Jin or not.

Jin: Ok. Fine. Here's what we do. Cut through the fence. Go in. Search the storage unit. What do you think? I'll be your right-hand man. Literally. LOL

Me: I need a left hand.

Jin: Whatever. What do you think of my plan?

It's not a bad plan exactly. And I don't have an alternative to offer up.

Jin: Well??!?!??!

Me: Great plan.

Jin: I can't tell if you're kidding or not.

Neither can I.

The next morning in the cafeteria, over Redwood pancakes, which are as good as advertised, Jin attempts to convince me that we are not *actually* breaking into the storage locker.

"The way I see it," he explains, tucking into his second helping, "your legal guardian owns the storage unit. And you can't get arrested for breaking into your own house."

"What?" I'm too busy swooning over breakfast to really pay attention.

"Irma. She's like family," he repeats.

"She *is* family," I point out. "She's my father's aunt."

"You know what I mean."

"But remember, Irma hasn't paid the bills in four months, so it's possible Bay Area Mini Storage actually owns everything inside the locker. Like, repossession." In which case, we will be stealing. But Jin waves me off. He's completely rationalized this entire venture. He even thinks it will be fun. Like doing a puzzle or playing Uno. I don't have time to dissuade him of this notion because

Hannah plunks her tray down on the table, orange juice sloshing out of the glass and all over everything.

"What are you talking about?" Hannah asks. She dumps a liter of syrup on her pancakes. It cascades down the sides like lava from an active volcano. "Who's breaking in where?"

Jin gags on his sausage patty. "Huh?" Hannah was on the *other side* of the room when Jin mentioned breaking and entering. There is no way she overheard us unless she has superpowers. Which is something I do not want to consider.

"*Who* is breaking and entering?" she says again, enunciating each word, to be sure we get it.

"No one," Jin says. But his lopsided grin is all wrong and Hannah focuses on him with laserlike intensity. Now we have problems.

"I *heard* you say breaking and entering," she says curtly. "And you are sitting with a known criminal."

Jin turns to me. "Hannah has no filter," he explains sweetly. "Whatever comes into her brain comes out her mouth. It's tragic."

"Don't make me go tell the Jelly," she says.

"But we haven't done anything!" Jin protests.

"It's only a matter of time," she replies. "Confess or the Jelly."

Neither of those are good choices. It's a moment for the

time-honored tactic of misdirection. Look this way while I do something that way that I don't want you to see. "Do you guys have any idea how scary it is to fall out a second-story window?" I blurt, holding up my arm and twirling it around. Hannah spins in her chair, glancing at the disintegrating green cast. Works every time.

"Rumor has it that you almost made a clean getaway," she says. "But took a header into a fountain and got caught."

While fountains are more glamorous than rosemary hedges, this is not exactly the turn in conversation I was hoping for. All eyes on me, expectant. Are they waiting on the real story? Uh-oh. "The judge asked me not to disclose the details."

"Like a gag order?" Hannah presses. Why won't she just eat her pancakes and leave me alone? "Are you a spy? A government agent? CIA? NSA? Undercover FBI?"

"What? No!"

"Oh look!" Jin leaps to his feet, tapping his watch. "We're supposed to see Mr. Miller before class, Lola. *Remember?* Come on!" His misdirection is way better than mine.

"But you don't have Mr. Miller this year." Hannah narrows her gaze, suspicious.

"Minor details!" Before I can even finish my food, Jin drags me away from the table and out of the cafeteria. But

I'm fully aware of Hannah's eyes boring into my retreating back. When we are safely behind the library, Jin stops and wipes his sweaty forehead on his sleeve.

"That was close." We backtrack around the library and head for our lockers, keeping an eye out in case we have to dodge Hannah. "But let's talk about the plan for tonight. I've added some details. After we cut the fence, we use Frank to blast our way into the unit. We can blow the door right off the place! What do you think?"

I'm glad he didn't mention Paul and being bad at ideas. That feels like progress. However, the plan stinks. "No. And . . . just no."

"Well, I'm just brainstorming here," Jin says defensively, a flash of hurt visible in his dark eyes.

The bell rings for class, giving me a jolt. I hoist my math text into my backpack and dig through the locker debris for a decent pencil with a point. Stuff starts falling out. How can my locker be such a mess in less than a week? I cram everything in and shoulder it closed. It takes a few tries, which is why I don't really notice Hannah, mere feet away, jotting something down in her notebook and grinning wildly.

CHAPTER 12

BREAK-IN BEFORE BREAKFAST

AFTER SCHOOL EMILY PICKS ME UP TO TAKE ME TO the doctor to get a new cast. She has been fully briefed on my volcano mishap. But while Irma did not ask a lot of follow-up questions, Emily's job is to be suspicious of my behavior.

"Just how did you ruin the cast?" she asks, clutching the steering wheel so tightly I can see her knuckle bones. "I'd like you to walk me through it, step by step."

I explain exactly what would have happened had we been building a baking soda volcano, taking care to empha-size how this was for school and would not have happened if I weren't trying to be a good student.

"Isn't that what you want?" I ask. "The STEM fair is important and I want to be a part of it. I have a partner and everything."

"You're making friends?" Emily asks tentatively, as if afraid of the answer.

"Yes." No reason she needs to know the specifics of my arrangement with Jin. Why upset her?

"So this damaged cast was *really* an accident?"

"I was at Jin's house," I point out. "Look, I understand this is my last chance to go straight and I take that very seriously."

Emily throws me a sideways glance. I may have laid it on a bit too thick with the "last chance" part. But Emily relaxes her grip on the wheel. She stretches her neck side to side, releasing the buildup of tension. She believes me. I have averted plunging through the very thin ice. For now.

That night, admiring my brand-new shocking pink cast, I form a real plan with Jin. We do this entirely on EmoJabber, which means I don't actually know what the plan is. I think we are supposed to show up at the bus stop midway between our houses at five o'clock in the morning; however, I might have agreed to ride a dragon to the outer rim for all I know.

But right on time the next morning, Jin runs up to the bus stop like his hair is on fire, eyes blazing. "It was all going so well," he says, breathless, "until Bart almost caught me! Do you know what my life would be *like* if Bart had a secret on me?" I've only met Bart once, but I imagine the answer to this question is completely intolerable. "Anyway, I want to go on record as saying I'm super excited and sick to my stomach at the same time. Can that even happen?"

Yes. I know this from experience. The bus glides into the stop, rumbling and backfiring, and the driver doesn't even raise an eyebrow when we board. It is very easy to be invisible in a city. We take a seat toward the front, lugging enormous backpacks stuffed with uniforms and school-work for later. It is not ideal for a break-in, but timing is important here. We cannot be late for first period.

Bay Area Mini Storage is nestled among a series of waterfront warehouses. No one lives in this neighborhood. A drift of morning fog hangs low, upping the creepiness factor. Jin looks queasy, gulping at the chilly air.

"Relax," I urge. "If we get caught, just let me do the talking."

"Absolutely," Jin says quickly. "Good idea."

I pick a spot along the fence far from the small security-guard shed near the entrance and between two surveillance cameras. Here's what I've learned about surveillance cameras in my short life of crime—they are only as good as the people watching them, and most of the time, those people are asleep.

Squatting by the fence, I pull a pair of wire cutters from my backpack. Jin yelps at the sight of them. "Be quiet," I hiss.

"Sorry," he mumbles. "Just, you know, we're really *doing* this. Are you afraid of anything, Lola?"

"Some stuff."

"You don't seem like you are."

Honestly? Rats. I really don't like them. "How about you close your eyes? And I will tell you when it's over."

"Good idea." Jin squeezes his eyes shut, which makes him a poor candidate for lookout, although there is not much to see in the foggy darkness. He keeps his eyes shut even as he helps me awkwardly squeeze the wire cutters. This cast is a huge drag.

Finally, we manage to cut a square in the fence big enough for us to wiggle through. It's remarkable no one loses a finger. I elbow Jin to open his eyes and beckon him to follow me through the hole. On the other side, we scurry to the first building for cover and wait breathlessly to see if sirens begin to blare. My heart flutters like a panicky chicken in my chest. Jin, huddled behind me, shakes.

But nothing happens. No one is paying attention. How great is *that*? We huddle against unit number twenty-seven, meaning seventeen should be on the other side.

"Ready?" I whisper. Jin nods silently. I've never heard him so quiet. I hope he hasn't lost the capacity for speech due to abject fear. I'd feel bad about that. Quickly, we hustle around to the other side of the building and there is unit number seventeen. The garage-style door is secured with a big shiny padlock. It looks brand-new, like someone just recently put it on the door. I pull on it just to make sure it's not somehow magically unlocked. Nope.

I couldn't find a crowbar in Irma's backyard toolshed and, besides, it would definitely look suspicious hanging out of my backpack. Instead, I pull out a large flathead screwdriver. Standing before that heavy lock, I have my doubts that even with three good hands we can bust it open.

"Do you have the key?" Jin croaks.

"You're okay!" I'm so glad he's not scared speechless anymore I want to hug him. But his expression says I better wait on that.

"The key," he repeats. "To *open* the lock. You had to know there would be a lock. Did you even look?"

I glance skyward. "Well . . ."

"You don't do things the easy way, do you?" Jin whispers. It's true that even when I search for the shallowest part of the stream, I often fall in over my head anyway. Jin sighs. "If we don't have a key, we need leverage. A rock or something to use as a fulcrum for the screwdriver."

"Good idea." I scurry away to the edge of the fencing and come back with a fist-size chunk of broken concrete. Jin wedges the head of the screwdriver into the lock and props the concrete under the handle. Slowly, he presses down. The metal scratches the concrete, making an awful racket that will surely wake everyone within a five-mile radius, including the security guard snoozing in his shed. But Jin gives the screwdriver one final push and, just like that, the lock springs open. Stunned, Jin lets the concrete chunk drop to the ground.

"It worked?" He gazes at the lock. "It worked!"

"We just made our own luck," I say with appropriate awe.

"Let me guess. That's something your dad always says."

"Yup. Help me get it open." We struggle to raise the garage-style door about two feet before shoving our packs under and rolling into the unit. Jin flips a light switch and there is the unmistakable patter of little feet fleeing. *Rats.* The little hairs at the back of my neck immediately stand on end.

Everything inside is covered in a fine layer of dust. Cobwebs stretch across the corners. Rabbit-size dust bunnies drift along the floor. Large moving boxes are stacked along the back wall, with BENKO scrawled on the cardboard in my father's familiar sloppy handwriting. And suddenly it makes sense. This is *our* storage locker, junk left over from the time before we lived out of suitcases and duffel bags. Irma must have been handling the details because we never had an address, and I'm willing to bet that a few months ago, she promptly forgot it existed.

My father's desk and chair are shoved up against the back wall. I have a memory of watching him at that desk, head down, muttering to himself, writing frantically as if possessed. But this must have been before my mother left because after that, we never stopped moving from place to place. There was no desk and no chair. The dust makes my eyes water.

"Are you okay?" Jin rests a hand on my shoulder.

I blink rapidly. "Yeah. Good. Let's see if there's any treasure lying around." The sooner we find something, the faster we can get out of here. But only because of the rats.

CHAPTER 13

DEFINE "VALUABLE."

THE FIRST BOXES I YANK OPEN ARE FILLED WITH stacks of the pocket-size red leather notebooks my father fills with the agonizing details of every treasure-hunting expedition he ever went on. I shove the boxes aside. These notebooks are *not* valuable. They are boring with a capital *B*.

There's a box with pencil sharpeners, scissors, hole punches, melted glue sticks, and bags of dusty old pens. Also *not* valuable. A set of chipped dinner plates and an entire box of mismatched glasses? Not valuable and not valuable. Two boxes are filled with mail addressed to Dad, care of Irma Benko, and another with moldy paperback books and coiled extension cords. There's an old stepladder and several rolled-up carpets, where I'm sure the rats are living very happily with their extended rat families. Jin holds up a cardboard shoebox. It looks heavy.

"Rocks," he says flatly.

"Like, literally?" I peer into the box. Maybe there is a diamond hidden in there. I'll also take rubies, sapphires, or emeralds. I'm not picky. We dump the box on the floor and poke through it. The rocks are all different shapes and shiny, the kind you'd use to make a patio mosaic. Maybe Great-Aunt Irma had big plans and then decided the backyard was too far out of her comfort zone? Jin plucks out an iridescent green one, rounder than the rest, which fits nicely in the palm of his hand.

"Pretty," he says, admiring it. Yes, but that doesn't help us.

"Not valuable," I say with a sigh, shoving the rocks back into the box. Is a two-pound emerald so much to ask? We move on with our search. Jin produces a set of tarnished candlesticks from the next box.

"Valuable?" he asks.

"Not valuable." There is nothing here but useless junk, castoffs from a life that Dad and I stopped living long ago. My heart sinks.

"Lola?"

"Jin?"

"You look weird. Is it the rats?"

I jump up from my position squatting over a box of *National Geographic* magazines from 1989. "Why? Do you see rats?"

"No."

I exhale sharply. "Okay. Good."

"But I hear them."

"Can we please hurry *up*?"

We dig through the remaining boxes at lightning speed, tossing up clouds of dust. Our prospects dim with each new box we open until Jin waves me over. "Look at this. It's addressed to you." He peers into a tall box, covered in foreign postage and inky custom stamps, sealed with layers of grimy tape. Its journey was definitely a long one. My name is scrawled across the front in Dad's messy handwriting.

"We better open it," I say, my pulse quickening. Maybe Dad mailed me directions on how to find him? That would be helpful. Or valuable treasure? I'll take that, too. The dried-out tape disintegrates at our touch. Tentatively, I lift a box flap, almost afraid to look inside.

"What are you waiting for?" Jin asks. When I don't answer, he hip-checks me out of the way and throws open the top. "I don't know what it is, but it might be valuable."

I lean over and have a look. My whirligig! The one from the Coke cans I was building in Prague, right before Dad threw me on a plane to San Francisco and disappeared. He mailed it, just like he said he would. I blink a few times rapidly, running my sleeve over my eyes just to make sure nothing leaks out. Jin stares at me.

"I used to make these," I explain. "Wind spinners. Out of stuff I'd collect on our travels. This was my biggest one, but I never finished it." Gingerly, I lift it out of the box. Parts of it didn't survive the trip, but on the whole it's in pretty good shape.

"I like it," Jin says quietly.

"I don't make them anymore." Suddenly, I don't want to see it. It makes me sad in a way I don't have time for. "And it's not valuable. It's just more junk." I shove it back into the box. We never should have come here. I kick at a giant dust bunny on the floor. When my foot swings out, two little brown ears pop up from behind the box of *National Geographic* magazines.

A rat! Frantic, I upend the whirligig box as I scramble for purchase on the desk.

"It's just a rodent," Jin says with a snort. "It's not going to eat you."

"Is it gone?" I whisper.

He can't answer because he is doubled over with uncontrollable laughter and has to catch his breath. "Yes," he says finally.

"Good."

"What's your problem with rats? They're no big deal."

"Long story." And not one I am about to get into right now. Or ever. I jump down from the desk and set the whirligig box back to upright. "Let's go. I'm sorry I got you into this." Feelings roil in my chest that weren't there before.

"Hold on," says Jin. Something in his voice makes me freeze. Is there a rat close to me? On me? I break out in a cold sweat. "Under the desk."

Jin gets down on all fours to look under the desk. *What* is he doing? Is he insane? There are rats down there!

"Check it out." Blowing his wayward bangs out of his eyes, he holds up a brown paper–wrapped package, about the size of a book. "It must have fallen out of the box because it wasn't here a minute ago."

Oh, this is exciting! Maybe Dad really *did* send treasure. A priceless Gutenberg Bible or a first-edition *Canterbury Tales*? I grab the parcel. But before I can rip it open, there are footsteps outside on the concrete, headed in our direction. Fast. With purpose. Our slumbering security guard has awoken.

"Uh-oh," I say, jamming the parcel into my bag.

"What do we do?" Jin squeaks.

"When in doubt, run."

"Is that another one of your father's sayings?"

No. That one is all mine.

We grab our stuff and roll under the door. A flashlight beam sweeps by, just missing us. There's no time to secure the storage unit, not that we could anyway, having busted the lock clean off to get in.

"Hey!" shouts a booming voice. "Stop right there!" That is our invitation to sprint. We dash toward the hole in the fence as if our pants are on fire, Jin gasping, just behind me. But, man, this guy is fast. Too fast. He's on an electric scooter! Really, what are the chances?

I shove Jin through the hole, practically clubbing him with my cast, and climb through after him. We scramble to our feet and run. The man heaves the scooter through the opening and attempts to follow. His curses echo in the darkness as he gets hung up on the cut wire fencing.

"Is he coming?" Jin wheezes as we dash down the tree-lined road.

"No," I grunt. Yes. The flashlight beam is gaining on us. Suddenly, I have an idea. Grabbing Jin by the jacket, I bank a sharp right turn off the pavement and hunker down behind a crop of trees.

"What the—" I clamp my good hand over Jin's mouth before he gives up our position. Scooter Man slows down, tossing his slick silver ride to the curb.

"Come out, you little brats!" he bellows. "I *saw* you! Don't think you can get away with this!" He strides into the trees, coming right for us. I can practically hear Jin's heart pounding through his hoodie. Digging through the underbrush, I get my hands on a thick branch and hurl it away from us. It hits a pile of dry leaves. Scooter Man immediately turns toward the sound.

"Just give up already!" he shouts.

No. Way. I wait until his footsteps move off in the direction of the branch and, keeping a tight grip on Jin's jacket, I sprint for the scooter. I have no idea how to drive one, but how hard can it be? The answer is super easy with two hands and not easy at all with one. Jin, riding behind me, howls as we veer wildly toward a parked car. Scooter Man is hot on our trail again, waving his arms and screaming, but without his ride, he doesn't stand a chance. The wind blows through my hair as we disappear in the fog. Jin, arms around my waist, face plastered against my backpack, holds on for dear life.

We ride the scooter until it conks out. I lean it gently against a lamppost and we continue on foot to the nearest bus stop, where we sit on a damp bench in a dim pool of yellow light and catch our breath.

"We just made a getaway on an electric scooter," Jin says after a moment.

"We did," I confirm.

"I've never done that before."

"Me either."

"It was kind of cool," he says thoughtfully. "I don't want to do it again or anything, but you know what I mean."

"I do."

"Anyway, thanks for including me."

"I couldn't have done it without you," I say.

"Really?"

"It's the truth."

He hides a smile, his cheeks glowing with pride, and I think maybe he believes me at least a little bit.

"Let's look at that package," I say. I pull it out and tear into the brown paper wrapping, dropping it like confetti, only to reveal a sharp red corner. I know immediately what it is. My eyes blur. I wipe them on the back of my sleeve, quickly, before Jin notices.

"What?" Jin studies me.

"Nothing. It's just another stupid notebook. The kind my father used on expeditions. It's *not* valuable." My shoulders sag. "I'm sorry I dragged you into this."

"It was my idea, remember?" Jin grabs the book from my lap and pages through it. "Are you sure there are no treasure maps in here? You know, where *X* marks the spot?"

And just like that, my tired brain belches something useful to the surface. "Wait a minute. Star and Fish *asked* me about Dad's notebook. The first time I met them. They asked twice!"

"Huh?"

"The State Department agents! They wanted to know where the notebook was. Right after they told me I was an orphan. It was terrible bedside manner."

I grab the notebook back and hold it right up to my nose. It doesn't look any different from all the other ones, but it *must* be. Otherwise, why did the State Department agents want it? I flip quickly through the pages. They are all intact. Nothing appears to be missing.

A shadow falls on the pavement in front of us. It's long, twisted, and shaped like a Martian. When I look up, there is Hannah Hill, wearing her uniform and a sly grin. "Wow," she says. "You two have had a *busy* morning."

When encountering the unexpected, smile and pretend everything makes perfect sense until you figure out what is actually going on. That might be something my father says. Or maybe I just made it up.

CHAPTER 14

CAT AND MOUSE, SO WHICH ONE AM I?

UNINVITED, HANNAH WEDGES HERSELF IN BETWEEN us on the narrow bench. She is much too happy for this early hour.

Jin eyes her. "Are you *following* us?"

"Think about it," she says, as if we are complete idiots. "You two team up for the STEM fair and then I bust you talking about breaking and entering and *then* I overhear you at the lockers discussing the details of said breaking and entering and the location, so I tagged along." She pulls out a pair of binoculars and waves them around. "Got here before you and just kept an eye on things. Didn't even break a sweat. Although I thought you might be done for when the guard caught on. That was exciting, wasn't it?"

Jin's jaw hangs open. Hannah eyes him. "Come *on*," she says. "You would have done the same."

Jin does not appreciate being compared to Hannah Hill especially *by* Hannah Hill. "Are you kidding me?" he shrieks. "I would never do that. You're worse than my little brother!"

"NASA summer camp is on the line," she snaps. "You guys are up to something and I want to know what it is. So, tell me. Because I don't want to have to report to the Jelly what I see here, which is a common criminal and a loser, up to no good."

Wait a minute! I was willing to give her the benefit of the doubt, despite being Jin's nemesis and all, but now she's just being mean. My skin prickles with heat, but I smile benignly as I try to slip the notebook out of view. "We were out for a morning jog," I say. "To get in better shape."

"Fitness," Jin agrees. "It's important."

Hannah clears her throat. "You should remember that all actions have *consequences*."

The notebook is securely under my right thigh. "I think she's threatening us," Jin says. "Lola, do you think Hannah is threatening us?"

"I do. And I'm pretty sure the Redwood Academy code of conduct says 'No threatening other students.'"

Jin snorts. Hannah jumps to her feet, cheeks flushed, ready to throw down. But before this gets out of hand, the bus rolls up to the curb to save us. Quickly, I try to move the red notebook from under my thigh to my backpack, but I'm not so good at doing things with my right hand and it tumbles to the ground, falling at Hannah's feet, open to a page covered in scribbled notes and rudimentary illustrations. Hannah scoops up the book so fast I barely have time to register that I've lost control of it.

"Is this what you were after?" she asks. She studies the page intently, turning it this way and that. "A notebook?"

"No," I respond, swiping it back. "It's nothing. It's private."

Hannah gives me that sly smile again. "We'll see."

And I'll admit, my blood runs a little cold.

Back at Redwood, I really want to run directly to the library, find a quiet place, and *read* the notebook. If the State Department agents were so keen to get it, it must contain something of value. It might even tell me where my father *is*. Or at least where he was. This idea leaves me breathless. It means I'd have a place to *actually* start my search. I'm not sure I can survive another minute *not* knowing. However, after this morning's escapades, the thin ice under my feet feels especially squishy. I *cannot* skip class. The notebook will have to wait a little while longer.

I stuff the red book in my locker under textbooks for World History and Math 3. I add a box of highlighters on top. If anyone tries to swipe the notebook, they will be avalanched by school supplies. As the final bell rings for first period, I slam the locker shut and head off to French class, hopeful the rumors about éclairs are true because I'm starving.

The day is long. I can't think about anything but the notebook because I'm 100 percent sure the notebook will reveal all about what happened to my father. I'm so distracted I get conked on the head during dodgeball. After the last bell of the day, I find Jin pacing in front of my locker.

"Hurry up," he whispers. "Let's *go*." The plan is to take the notebook to the library. Under pressure, I forget my locker combination and Jin's head almost explodes. When the locker finally pops open, I prepare myself for the usual tumble of stuff, but nothing falls out. I peer inside. My locker looks almost . . . neat?

"Jin," I say, nudging him. "My locker. It's, like, *clean*." He takes a quick look, shrugs, grabs the notebook, and takes off down the hallway. I guess he doesn't care about the condition of my locker. I take off after him.

It's the moment of truth.

CHAPTER 15

ANY TIME IS A GOOD TIME FOR DOUGHNUTS.

WE HEAD TO THE LIBRARY BY WAY OF THE CAFETERIA because after school in the cafeteria there are doughnuts. Doughnuts! Glazed, sugar, sprinkles, jelly-filled, cream-filled, chocolate. Let me tell you, there are *no* good dough-nuts in Ulaanbaatar. This is exactly what Judge Gold was counting on. I'd become so distracted by Redwood, nothing else would matter. Doughnuts. How subversive. I take three.

We smuggle our sugary haul into the library right under the sign that says NO FOOD ALLOWED. I get the feel-ing Jin has done this before. There are a bunch of rainbow-colored beanbags near a big window on the second floor.

We plop down on two right next to each other and pull out the notebook. But my nerves are jangly, electric. Maybe it's all the sugar?

"What?" Jin asks.

"I'm kind of nervous," I confess. An idea that I have refused to consider even for a second pushes in around the edges. What if it turns out that I really am an orphan? What if everything those State Department agents told me is true? What happens *then*?

"I'm nervous too," Jin says quickly. "Actually, I'm completely freaking out."

Somehow being nervous together makes it seem all right. I take a deep inhale and flip open the cover of the notebook, promptly covering it with red jelly. Great. I'm going to smear up vital evidence with doughnut filling.

The first page indicates that Dad started using this notebook eight months ago. It includes the expedition name.

The Hunt for the Stone of Istenanya.

Huh?

"Your face is weird and we're only on the first page," Jin offers.

I point to the name. "The story of Istenanya is a fairy tale," I explain. "The stone is not a *real* thing. It's not something you go *hunt* for because it doesn't exist."

"Maybe it's code? Read!"

I clear my throat.

"'I am far behind. There is much to do if I'm to keep the stone from the hands of the mysterious Shadow.'"

"Stop!" Jin's doughnut is suspended in midair. "Who's the Shadow?"

"How am I supposed to know? He's mysterious!"

"Right. Okay. Go on."

"'The Task Force did not anticipate this turn of events, so they were woefully unprepared.'"

"Stop!"

"What now?"

"Who's the *Task* Force?"

I glare at him. "If you don't be quiet, I'm going to read to myself." He crams the rest of his doughnut in his mouth as a deterrent. I continue.

"'The Shadow is a new adversary, and although no one wants to admit it, he took us by surprise. He seems to have limitless resources and determination. While the Task Force races to identify him, it is up to me to stop him dead in his tracks. Right now he's breathing down my neck, but I can't be deterred. I'm organizing and making plans. Everything depends on my success!'"

I glance at Jin. He's riveted. He has no idea how boring

Dad's expedition notebooks normally are, which makes this one wildly unusual already. A secret Task Force and an adversary called "the Shadow"? But everyone *likes* Dad. He doesn't have enemies. And he works for himself, taking on expeditions for universities or museums or whoever is searching for lost things. I have never heard him mention a Task Force. I read on.

"'The clues I found in the Prague archives were remarkable, my first big break. But there's no time to bask in the glory. Next I need to get my hands on the maps and notes held at the university in Budapest. I've sent word to the librarian that I will be there tomorrow, but if this bad weather doesn't clear, I'll be stuck, sinking my efforts before I even get started. On the following pages, I've written everything I can remember about the stone from over the years. It's not much, but it's a start.'"

Why does he keep talking about the stone as if it's a *real* thing? The Shadow is not the only mysterious thing here. Breathlessly, I turn the page, anxious to understand what my father was thinking.

Imagine my surprise when there is nothing there, no more pages.

There is something Dad says when things go wrong, like when we run out of gas or the place he thought was a pharaoh's tomb turns out to be a landfill. It's not a nice thing, but I utter it anyway. Jin agrees wholeheartedly.

"But the pages were there when we found the book." I groan. "It was intact."

"Hannah," Jin snarls.

"Really? She'd do that?" Boy, if this is true, she might become my nemesis too.

"Totally. No question."

"*That's* why my locker was so organized. She stole the notebook and cleaned up."

"I can't believe she ripped out the pages." Jin fumes. "How dare she violate a *book*? That's, like, the worst! I bet she's at home right now gloating. We need to know who the evil Shadow is! And the Task Force! This is bad. What do we do?"

We can't confront her and demand the pages back. She will deny having them, and the only way to prove she does have them will be to reveal the existence of the notebook, which we don't want to do because that will require an explanation of how we got it. We have no choice but to take back what is rightfully ours.

"The answer is obvious," I say. "We steal them back."

Surprisingly, Jin grins. "Excellent."

Great. I have created a monster.

CHAPTER 16

BEGINNER'S LUCK

THE NEXT MORNING AT REDWOOD, I HAVE A HALF-formed, not very good plan to retrieve the pages when Jin tells me he has it all figured out. "I know *exactly* what to do," he says confidently.

"You do?" I remember that his last plan was, you know, not so amazing. But his confidence is growing like a parched plant that just got watered, so I swallow down my skepticism. "Go on."

"I've been going over it all night. It's easy, assuming Hannah hasn't recycled the pages or hidden them under her mattress, *and* she really is the one who stole them in the first place."

"That's a lot of assumptions," I point out.

But Jin tells me to relax and not worry. "I've got this. I promise. I'll see you back here after final bell." And without giving me any details, he saunters off to class like he is a master criminal, shoulders back, head high, fist-bumping every kid he passes.

Later, in ceramics, elbow-deep in clay, I work on a plan B because, while I like Jin's budding confidence, I estimate his chance of success to be somewhere around 3 percent. My plan involves finding out where Hannah lives and climbing through an open window. Unless she lives on the top floor of an apartment building, in which case I will hang around the entrance until someone comes out and I'll slip inside. No one is ever suspicious of kids. And I need those pages. What if they have what I'm looking for, a clue to my father's whereabouts? I'm so preoccupied my pot spins off the wheel and flies into the wall. My teacher is not pleased. My potentially glorious pot is now a misshapen mess. She tells me to stop daydreaming and start over. I take this as a bad omen.

When the bell finally rings one thousand years later, I leap from my potter's stool and fly out the door without even washing my hands. There are bits of gray clay under my fingernails and smears of it up my arms.

Jin waits in the hallway. "What's in your hair?"

"Clay," I say. "What's the plan? And I want details."

"Check this out." He clears his bangs from his eyes. "Hannah plays chess every Wednesday at Over the Hill Pizza, down in the Mission. It's, like, her and all these old guys, but apparently, she never misses it. My sources say she goes there *a lot*."

"Chess?"

"Yeah. The game? Jeez, you have to know what that is, right?"

Just because I didn't have an EmoJabber handle until a few days ago does not mean I grew up on Mars. I know what chess is. "Go on," I say flatly.

"Anyway, we *follow* her." He grins. I think he thinks he's invented the concept of trailing a person of interest.

"And?"

"Think about it." He arches a single eyebrow. "Most things of value in our lives are stuffed in our backpacks. I mean, I have a toothbrush in there. And extra shoelaces. And a bunch of granola bars. Basically, I could be left on a desert island with only my backpack and I'd be fine. Ergo, the pages must be in her pack. I like that word, don't you? It means therefore."

"I *know* what it means," I snap. Jin wants the pages to

be in Hannah's backpack; ergo, he is making yet another giant assumption. I'm developing a stomachache. "So?"

"So while Hannah is occupied playing chess, we sneak in, take the pack, swipe the pages, return the bag, and *leave*. Like I said. Easy!"

He layers on the details. He causes a distraction. I take the pack. I dig through it. I steal back the pages. I return the pack. Do you see where this is going?

"What do you think?" he asks breathlessly. I think his plan stinks. But is mine any better? It pains me to admit that it is not.

"Great," I say with a grimace. "Let's go get pizza." We catch a bus, spend the entire time hypothesizing about the true identities of the Shadow and the Task Force, and almost miss our stop on Valencia Street, in the heart of the Mission district. The street teems with people, eating, shopping, hanging around. Everyone seems to have a little dog or a bushy beard. Or both. There is a lot of purple hair and people in tank tops showing off tattoos, even though it is freezing and windy. Four blocks later, we stand in front of Over the Hill Pizza, a shabby restaurant with windows so thick with grime we can't see inside. Shouts echo from the propped-open door. We peer through, careful to keep ourselves out of view.

In the back there is a large pizza oven. A fog of cooking smoke hangs low. One woman, in a hairnet and a red shirt, mans the counter and the cooking. She tosses a circle of pie dough into the air, catching it and expanding it a few times before plopping it on a silver pizza pan.

A narrow hallway runs along the far side of the kitchen, probably leading to the bathrooms. About halfway down the hallway are a row of pegs laden with jackets and baseball caps. In the main section of the restaurant are eight small tables at which sit pairs of people, heads bent over chessboards. Lots of gray hair and wrinkles. And Hannah with her back to us. We ease away from the door.

"She's in there," Jin says triumphantly. "Good intel, right?"

"You want a trophy?"

"Maybe."

"Fine. After we get the pages."

"That's the easy part."

"Your inexperience is showing," I say.

"You're just jealous because you didn't think of this plan first."

For the record, I am *not* jealous. Hannah's Redwood uniform jacket hangs on one of the pegs, her backpack slung over it haphazardly. I nudge Jin and point. If he heads to the counter to order a slice, I can slip down the hallway undetected. My stomach rumbles, excited by the prospect of pizza. Not now, stomach. I'm busy.

"Act casual," Jin says as we enter the pizzeria. But his hands are balled into fists and he frowns. He doesn't move. I give him a shove. Stumbling, he cuts through the tables, headed for the counter. He pulls out his phone, pretending to be immersed in EmoJabber or whatever.

"Oops," he says, plowing right into the back of Hannah's chair. When she reels around to see who it is, I dash into the hallway, swipe her blue-and-yellow backpack, and beeline for the tiny bathroom. Sweat blooms on my forehead. Safely locked inside, I dump the contents of the pack on the gritty floor.

Wow. Hannah has a lot of stuff. ChapStick, hair elastics, ribbons, a sock, two empty water bottles, a wrinkled hoodie, three textbooks, miscellaneous notebooks, wads of crumpled-up paper, and three small bags of Doritos that I think seriously about eating. She'd be fine on that desert island. I sort through the debris. Nothing. I open all the pockets. Nothing. I turn the pack upside down and give it a vigorous shake. Dust and a few pebbles but no missing pages. Where did she stash them? In her locker? In her house? Jin's assumptions were dead wrong. Why did I let him run this operation in the first place? Sitting on the closed toilet, I take a moment to wonder why things *never* break my way.

"Is it wrong to want just a *little* luck?" I ask the empty bathroom. I mean, I ruined the sculpture, broke my wrist, and stabbed myself in the butt. Wouldn't just *one* of those misfortunes have gotten the message across? Why is my karma so compromised? What does the universe want from me? I resolve to be nicer to Zeus. Maybe that will help.

I'd like to wallow a few more minutes in my misfortune, but realistically, how long can I leave Jin unattended before something really bad happens out there? Quickly, I stuff everything back into the backpack and zip it closed. Reversing my actions, I return the bag to the peg and slip out of the shop. Or that's what I see myself doing. Unfortunately, just before my stealthy exit, my feet tangle in a chair and I stumble to the ground. Everyone stares. Jin shakes his head, disappointed. My cheeks flame red.

"Lola, too? *What* are you guys doing here?" She glances around, obviously dismayed, as if to make sure there are no other Redwood students lurking in the shadows, waiting to ambush her. Is it because we caught her playing chess? Whatever it is, she's not happy.

"Oh, Lola loves chess too," Jin blurts. "A ton. It's her favorite."

What? No, I don't. As I slowly return to my feet, humiliation burns inside my chest. This is all Dad's fault. I would not be here if he didn't go and get himself disappeared like he did.

"You play?" Hannah asks skeptically.

"No," I say quietly. "I just heard the pizza was . . . really good."

The lady in the red shirt with the hairnet steps out from behind the counter and strides toward us. The name "Maria" is embroidered above her pocket. "You heard right," she says, smiling. There is a gap between her teeth wide enough to suck spaghetti through. "The pizza is *outstanding*. Hannah, are these your school friends? Hannah *never* brings her school friends around. Do you want a slice? It will change your world."

Hannah drops her forehead to the table. "*Mom*."

Oh, I get it. Over the *Hill* Pizza. Duh. Jin is a little slower. "Wait a minute. This is *your* pizza place? I had no idea."

"That's because Hannah never brings anyone here. I don't get it. *Everyone* likes pizza." Her fingers drift to Hannah's long hair, unconsciously combing out knots that are probably not even there. But I get it. Sometimes the circumstances of our lives are embarrassing and usually there is nothing we can do about it but hope no one finds out. I've been in a lot of places where people looked at me funny.

Hannah shakes her mother's fingers from her hair. "These aren't my friends," she snaps. "They're just . . . kids from school."

But Maria isn't listening. "Did you know Hannah is going to win a trip to NASA this summer?" she says to us. "And then it's a straight shot to a Stanford scholarship! My girl is going to be a scientist and *change* the world." Maria swells with pride. And it's clear the worst thing Hannah could do is say she wants to make pizza for the rest of her life.

"Mom."

"Oh, I know you don't like me bragging on you, but sometimes I just can't help it."

"No. That's not it. Your pizza's on fire." Smoke billows from the oven.

"Oh no!" Maria rushes off to put out the flames.

As soon as she is out of earshot, Hannah turns to us, stuck somewhere between mortified and furious. "I don't know what you two are doing here, but you can go now."

Jin gives me an enthusiastic slap on the back. "Well, this has been fun, but you're right, we really should go." With some overly dramatic waving, he pulls me out of the pizzeria like the place is on fire, which it might actually be. Hannah's eyes stay on us as we retreat.

Walking fast, we put space between us and Over the Hill, talking over each other as we go. "Did you know her mom owned a pizza place?"

"Can you believe she had the nerve to say she didn't know what we were doing there? I mean, how could she *not* know?"

On the one hand, I see why Hannah can't take her foot off the gas. Maria has expectations and Hannah intends to meet them, exceed them, and then crush them, just to be sure. That kind of effort doesn't leave much time for fun, outside of chess matches with old guys. But on the other hand, she stole my pages. And we failed to get them back.

Beside me, Jin grins like the cat who ate the canary, although Great-Aunt Irma is not fond of that particular idiom. Why is he so happy? This is no time to be happy. The pages might be gone forever. We might never find out who the Shadow is.

"Stop smiling. The pages weren't in her backpack."

But he's not listening. He's dancing around on the sidewalk like he's got ants crawling all over him. "You were brilliant!" he shouts. "It's like you read my mind when you fell on your face. How did you *know*?"

Wait. What? I didn't trip on purpose. I wouldn't do that. The floor was disgusting.

"The minute you got Hannah's attention," he continues, flushed with excitement, "BOOM! I got the pages!" Jin holds up a wad of papers, my father's messy handwriting clearly in view. "Took them right from her sweater pocket! She had no idea!"

Hannah had the pages in her pocket. Jin saw an opportunity and took it. He didn't get caught. It is not lost on me that I have successfully achieved what I set out to do twice in the past eight months. The first time was the storage unit. The second time was just now. Both times with Jin.

Beginner's luck?

Or maybe he's just good at this.

CHAPTER 17

THE STONE OF ISTENANYA

WITH THE PAGES SECURE, WE SET OUT FOR JIN'S house, which is closest. I stay quiet as he relives his glory, again and again and *again*. You'd think two successful heists make him a legend from the way he goes on. He's not the one who got away with five hundred million in stolen paintings. I wish he'd stop gloating. He's insufferable. No wonder Paul moved away. When he asks me what's the matter, I mutter something about being hungry. And annoyed. And possibly just the tiniest bit jealous. The fact that he thinks I purposely fell down so he could snatch the pages undetected just makes me feel like more of a fraud.

Marco and Bart are at the house when we arrive,

playing checkers at the kitchen table. "I have lemon cake," Marco says enthusiastically. But when he invites us to sit down and talk about our day, Jin waves him off.

"Too much homework," he says. "STEM fair. Math sets. French vocabulary test." Vocabulary test? Really? "But we'll take the cake." He grabs two plates and a large hunk of cake, eliciting violent protests from Bart, who believes he is the rightful owner of at least half of what is left. Jin fends off his little brother and we head to the studio out back. I shake off my bad attitude. It's time to read the missing pages.

Taking seats on opposite sides of the long table, we smooth the crumpled papers flat. They aren't numbered and getting them into some coherent order takes time. Jin can't read my father's terrible handwriting and keeps putting the puzzle together the wrong way. By this point, the cake is mostly gone, which makes me sad.

Finally, we are ready to read. "Hurry up," Jin says. "I'm dying to know who the Shadow is. And the Task Force."

My stomach tightens around the cake. Jin makes it sound like a really good book or a show on television. But it's not. It's real life. He drums his fingers on the table. "Any day now, Lola."

Okay. Deep breath. Here we go.

"'The Shadow has thrown countless resources at

finding the stone, but the Task Force is limited. However, I'll do whatever it takes. The Shadow is sure to use the stone for evil, attempting world domination of the unwilling, including Lola. I can't let that happen. I must find the stone and protect it with my life. Nothing else matters.'"

I pause. This does not sound good. This sounds dangerous. "He's talking about the stone again," Jin says. "The one you say doesn't exist."

I hold up my hands, confused. "It doesn't. The Stone of Istenanya is a story, a folktale. Not *real*."

"Like Cinderella?"

"Not exactly," I reply. "Well, not at all. Istenanya is a Hungarian goddess. She liked the mortals, you know, how gods sometimes do in mythology."

"Although it never works out well for the mortals," Jin points out. "Like the Greek gods. They were always turning the humans into trees and boars and stuff."

He's right. Never make friends with a god or goddess unless you are comfortable with transformation into a barnyard animal. "Istenanya believed that humans had good intentions," I explain, "but they struggled to do the right thing. The earth was a hot mess. War, death, disease. At least that's the way my mother used to tell the story."

"That sounds awful," Jin says. "What happened?"

"Well, the goddess searches far and wide and finds a *good* human."

"Someone who isn't a jerk?"

"Yeah. Probably someone with empathy and compassion and all that sort of stuff."

Jin nods. "Go on."

"So anyway, Istenanya finds this good human with compassion and empathy and gifts this person a stone, an emerald-green magic rock to be exact. It allows the good human to influence the thoughts of other people."

"Like mind control?" There is one bite of cake left on Jin's plate. I eye it. He slides it toward me.

"Sort of," I say, spraying cake crumbs all over the table. "Do you have any milk? A glass of milk would be good right now."

"Finish the story and I'll get you a glass of milk. You said mind control."

"Istenanya figured one good person able to influence others could create a domino effect of goodness. Or something like that. And then things on earth would improve."

"Well, *do* they?"

"Not exactly," I whisper.

"Not *exactly*?" Jin jumps to his feet, upturning the cake plate, which crashes to the floor.

"You need to calm down," I say. "It's only a story."

Jin points at the notebook. "It sure doesn't sound like your dad thought so."

"Milk?" I ask.

"Finish," Jin replies.

Boy, he's tough. "Okay, where was I? Right. Along comes the underworld god Ördög, who's a real beast, you know, bad hair, stinky breath, rotten teeth, warts, dirty fingernails, the works."

"Ördög is ugly. I get it. Go on."

"So Ördög *steals* the stone. He's dead set against giving the puny stupid humans a leg up. He thinks they are weak and should be left to destroy each other if that's what they want. They are not worthy of the godly power of the stone and Ördög intends to prove this to Istenanya, who he thinks is a hopelessly optimistic goddess. When Istenanya is off, I don't know, bathing in a babbling brook with her nymphs or whatever, Ördög imbues the stone with dark powers, turning Istenanya's experiment on its head. *Now* any mortal who possesses it can lead others to acts of great treachery and evil. It's like having a posse of zombies at the ready, to act out your worst impulses. He makes it so the stone seduces you into believing it's working for you when really it's biding its time before it can use you to perpetrate evil."

Jin has stopped breathing. He stares at me. "Did you say a zombie posse?" he whispers.

"Of course, like any fairy tale, there are tons of variations. They probably don't all have a zombie posse. Anyway, by the time Istenanya realizes what's happened, it's too late. The humans have the evil stone and they begin to do awful things, more awful than what they've been doing already. So, Istenanya appears among the mortals in disguise, steals back the stone, and hides it away for eternity. It's the least she can do after Ördög makes a total mess of things."

Jin considers this. "But if the stone *were* real," he says slowly, "it could be dangerous."

"Well, yeah. If it were real, it could pretty much end the world as we know it. Everyone would just be running around committing murder and mayhem and cutting in line and stealing and cheating and whatever. Just one person can poison the well."

Jin looks alarmed. "This is bad."

"But the stone isn't real!" I shout. "Didn't you hear anything I said? Istenanya is a fairy tale. There is no stone." There *can't* be.

Because a real stone could be real trouble.

CHAPTER 18

CRAZY OR CRAZY? TAKE YOUR PICK.

THE MOOD IN THE LITTLE STUDIO DARKENS. JIN frowns. I continue to read. Dad talks about how the Task Force mobilized him so quickly he barely had time to sort out his affairs, but the safety of the world was at stake. He had no option but to park me with Irma and find the stone. It's the only way to keep it safe. From what he writes, it's clear he thinks he's close to success.

For the record, I am *not* interested in saving the world. No way. I'm in it to find my father and get back to my life. By the last page of notes, Dad has traipsed all over Eastern Europe looking for an artifact that is not supposed to exist. He bounces from excited to despairing back to worried sick, where he is in the last written paragraphs.

"'The elders here in this tiny town warn me off the stone. They speak of a dark power that preys on people who are desperate, using their deepest desires against them. A white-haired man described how the stone's power hugs a person, clings to them, until it achieves its purpose and proves Ördög's point. Humanity is weak. It is not worthy of a goddess's help. They speak of how the stone chooses a person and whispers to them, like a shiver, as if a spirit is floating nearby. The stone calls out to its intended, a voice in the fog, dim, quiet, but persistent, insistent. It tells you it can help you, that it can make you whole if only you let it show you how. It then leads you on to great evil. Or this is what they say.

"'From the stories the elders weave, I've pieced together a rudimentary map of the stone's possible location. There is a mountain and a river, a tree and a cave. I recognize one of the references, a great old pine on a mountain path not terribly far from here. I believe I am the sole possessor of this knowledge, so I go tonight, still hopeful. Of course, who knows what will happen?

"'It's important that if I am lost, there is no record of what I'm doing here. This notebook will be in the mail to San Francisco by the time I leave. My greatest hope is to reunite with it, and Lola, in a few weeks' time.'"

My eyes water a little bit. There must be dust on the pages. This is not what I wanted to read. Is it possible Star and Fish were telling some part of the truth? Sure, they lied about the flash flood and all of that, but that's not the point. Maybe Dad went into the woods and never came out. But *where*? Which river? What mountains? I sigh, loud and deep.

"Why are you so droopy?" Jin demands. "We are hunting a magic stone! I have never done anything remotely this amazing in my entire life! We are *so* on this." He pulls out a notepad and a pencil. "Let's recap. Your father works for the secret Task Force, which sounds cool even if we have no idea what it is. He thinks the fairy-tale stone is real and he knows where it is. There's a bad guy named the Shadow who plans to use it to take over the world, specifics not included. Dad mails that notebook back here for safekeeping. Is that about it?"

"Yeah," I say, deflated. "But we have no idea where he was. Or if he found the stone. Or what happened next." Any of those bits of information would have put us ahead, but basically, we know nothing more than we did before, which means that for all our effort, we've gotten nowhere. I am right back at the beginning, desperately trying to find a way to Europe, where I will wander around cluelessly looking for my father.

"Your attitude is terrible," Jin chastises. "There are a number of possibilities. Maybe your dad found the stone and is in hiding from the Shadow. Maybe he's been holed up somewhere for eight months and doesn't have access to a phone. Or maybe his hiding place is in the middle of the ocean? Or the jungle? Or the desert? I'll tell you one thing. I always *thought* our world had magical powers. I just figured we were too stupid to figure out what they were and how to use them. So, this is cool. But also, not. Because we all know what happens when uncontrollable magic is unleashed on the world."

We do? A panicky little flutter lodges in my chest. I always have at least a vague idea of my next move. But right now I draw a complete blank. I have no idea what to do next.

CHAPTER 19

HANNAH KNOWS EVERYTHING.

THE NEXT DAY HANNAH WAITS BY MY LOCKER. I don't have time for her. I'm busy planning the theft of an albino penguin. I was sure the notebook was the key to finding my father, but now that I've had time to process how wrong *that* was, I'm ready to move on. The only way to find my father is to get out there in the world and start looking. The albino penguin will surely secure me the resources required to do just that. Today's goal is to figure out how to fence a penguin. How hard can it be?

"Excuse me," I say, shoving past Hannah. "I need my social studies homework."

"We need to talk," she says flatly. "I want in."

"Into *what*?" I'd be happy to push her into a toilet, if that's what she means. But alas, I don't think it is.

"The hunt for the magic stone," she hisses. "The one from the pages."

"The pages you *stole* from me," I remind her.

"I had no choice," she says, as if I am to blame. "I want in on the search for the Ishy whatever it is. You don't think I'm going to just let you two go off and make a potentially *magical* electromagnetic pulse generator, do you? No way. And just so we're clear, I can make your life miserable if you don't cooperate."

"It's called the Stone of Istenanya," I reply. "And it has nothing to do with the STEM fair!"

"You *say* that."

Exasperated, I throw up my hands. "Let's just say, hypothetically, that there *is* a hunt going on. Why would I let you in on it? You stole my pages!"

"Because otherwise I tell the Jelly what you guys were up to at Bay Area Mini Storage," she says bluntly.

She's trying to blackmail me. I can't believe it. "Go ahead. You have no proof." It would be her word against ours, and while I realize I have no credibility, Jin has plenty. I'm 80 percent sure he would emerge victorious.

"Don't I?" She pulls out a phone, not as sleek and new

as Jin's but decent enough to show a video clip of Jin and me cutting into the fence at Bay Area Mini Storage.

"You did not," I hiss.

"I did. And there is no way I let you two dorks go on a quest for the magical stone of whoever without *me*."

But here's the thing. If there is no hunt for a magical stone, there is nothing for her to join! Her blackmail is useless.

"Fine," I say. "You're in."

She takes a step back. "Really?"

"Really. I don't want to get Jin in trouble with that video."

Her eyes flash with concern. "I kind of thought you'd push back more. You know, negotiate."

I shrug. "I know when I'm beat."

"This is weird." She narrows her gaze, suspicious.

"I have to go to class."

"You promise, right?"

"Yup." I hold up my fingers to show none of them are crossed. "Can you move?"

"*Really* promise?"

"What do you want from me?" I shout, making her jump. "A blood oath? I promise. Okay? I get it. I remember. Now can you please move? I'm late."

Finally, she smiles and steps aside. "Excellent."

After classes, we head to the cafeteria for milkshakes before Jin's fencing practice and my return to the library for further penguin liberation research. Redwood Academy might be run by the Jelly, but the food is excellent. Misty fog settles over the campus like it does most afternoons. I button up my ugly red cardigan, but it doesn't help.

"Something happened," I say as we walk.

"I know! I heard that Bradley farted in Spanish class and Mathilda passed out from the stink. Gross."

That *is* gross. "No. Not that." I bring him up to speed on the Hannah blackmail video situation. He stops abruptly. His jaw drops open.

"You *promised* she could hunt for the rock with us?" he asks, aghast. Oddly, he seems less concerned with her turning us in to the Jelly than he does with a meaningless partnership. Which is irritating because I thought I played that one perfectly.

"We're hunting penguins," I remind him, "not rocks! I mean, not hunting, but you know what I mean."

Jin glares at me. "You underestimate Hannah at your own risk."

"It's not going to make any difference," I say crossly. "There's *no* quest." Before our argument can escalate, our path to the cafeteria is blocked by a woman in an outfit that was possibly barfed up by a rainbow. Her lipstick is bright red.

"Lola Benko," she purrs. "I've been looking everywhere for you."

For some reason, this doesn't feel like a good thing.

CHAPTER 20

LIPSTICK

THE LADY WITH THE BRIGHT RED LIPSTICK SEEMS vaguely familiar, but I can't figure out why. She wears dark sunglasses, her blond-and-purple streaked hair pulled back into a bun that stretches the skin on her face so tight, I swear I can see her skull. Her purple Converse sneakers match the color in her hair.

"Do you two know each other?" Jin looks from me to her and back again.

"In a way," Lipstick says. What the heck does that mean? Confused, I keep my mouth shut and wait for her to explain. "I work for an individual who wants the same thing *you* want. And my employer, for better or for worse, always gets what he wants."

Oh, this does not sound good. Jin nudges me with his elbow, but I'm afraid to even look at him.

"My employer's message for you, Lola Benko, is simple." Lipstick's face does not move when she talks, on account of the supertight bun. "You have forty-eight hours to produce the stone."

"Huh?"

"The *stone*," she repeats. "Don't play dumb with me. We know that you know that we know that you know where the stone is." Hold on. Who knows what exactly? "Bring it to us or you will never see your father again. Do you understand?"

Her words swirl around in my head like a tornado. My lips flap in the breeze, any response stuck fast in my throat. Jin hip-checks me. "Lola," he hisses. "Say something."

"He's *alive*?" I finally manage to whisper. My heart pounds wildly against my ribs. I think I might faint.

"For now," Lipstick says curtly. "What happens next depends on you. If you tell anyone, consequences. If you don't produce the stone, consequences. If you try to pull a fast one, consequences."

"But I don't know where the stone *is*," I blurt. Clearly,

my father found it and hid it and they think he told me where. But that stone might as well be a needle in a haystack with the haystack on Mars. "It could be anywhere!"

"That's a tired old line, kid," she replies with a sharp laugh. "Do you get what I'm saying or not?"

"I get it," I murmur. "Stone. Father. Consequences."

"Wow," whispers Jin. "This is getting seriously complicated."

"Once you have the stone, call me." Lipstick hands over an ordinary business card with a number on it. Nowhere on that card does it say "evil henchman" or "villain." And then she's gone, just like that.

I grab Jin by the shoulders. "My father is alive!"

He looks grave. "But I think he's been captured by the *Shadow*."

This is all too much. I start to cry. And Jin freaks out because I'm standing there weeping like a baby and we're not even friends. My father is *alive*! And now I have confirmation. But more important, *how* do I find the stone? This Shadow guy doesn't sound like a reasonable person at all. My emotions whiplash until I start to wobble. Jin loops his arm through mine to keep me steady.

"You were right." Jin hands me a crumpled tissue that probably has snot on it. "Honestly, when we first met, I thought you might be a little, you know, not thinking straight about your dad, but you were right." This just makes me cry harder. "Oh jeez, that was the wrong thing to say. Sorry. Ugh. Here, have more tissues."

He turns the pockets of his uniform jacket inside out and dumps the contents on the sidewalk—tissues, a pencil stub, a few sticky notes, two sticks of gum. He quickly gathers up the tissues and stuffs them in my hands. "Maybe gum will help?"

Get a grip, Lola! The clock is ticking. Forty-eight hours is not long to find something that is worse than lost, something that is not supposed to exist in the first place. But I have to *try*. With some effort, I rein in the cry fest. "We don't have much time." I sniffle.

"I think we need to go to the police right away," Jin says. "Or the FBI or whoever handles magical stones on Planet Earth. Because even if we do find it, obviously we can't just *give* it to the Shadow. He's the bad guy!"

This gets my attention. What is he talking about? "Of *course* we're going to give it to him. It's just a rock."

"Your dad doesn't think so," Jin says. "He was willing to do anything to protect the stone. He wrote that in his journal. Would he want you to just turn it over? The whole *point* was to keep it out of the Shadow's hands."

"Wait a minute," I interrupt. "Do you actually believe the stone has real magical powers?" Jin shrugs, noncommittal, but I can see it in his eyes. Just like for Hannah, my dad, and the Shadow, the *idea* of magic has him under a spell. What is *wrong* with everybody? "Well, it doesn't. It's just a stupid rock, one I need to get my father back."

"Lola, this is the *world* we're talking about." What is he implying? That it's selfish to be more concerned with the fate of one person than it is to consider the other seven billion? Well, I don't *know* the other seven billion, thank you very much.

"I don't care," I say.

"But your dad," Jin responds. "He didn't want—"

"It's not your father that's in trouble!" I yell.

Jin flinches. My cheeks flush hot. My hands ball into tight fists. How dare Jin, with his perfect family and cool work studio and bratty little brother, tell me what *my* father would want? Besides, I don't care what my father wants. I've been trying to find him for eight months and now I am so close. "You don't know anything about him," I hiss, "and you know nothing about me."

Jin steps back, stunned, as if I slapped him. "Whatever," he says after a pause. "Do what you want."

And with that, he peels off the path, leaving me

fuming. What is wrong with him anyway? I'm so mad I can't even hear my own thoughts. It's like a bunch of cats are crammed into my head, all howling for dinner. Finally arriving at the cafeteria, I can't bring myself to go in. Instead, I trudge back up the path to get my backpack and head home. It starts to rain.

Of course it does.

CHAPTER 21

A VERY BAD, TERRIBLE, AMAZING, CONFUSING DAY

ON THE WAY HOME, THE RAIN DRENCHES MY REDWOOD Academy skirt and wilts my crisp white shirt. Little rivers run down my back and water drips off the ends of my hair. I never said I had any interest in saving the world. I'm in this to get my father back and that's it. And the stone isn't magic, so who cares if the Shadow has it? I mean, the worst he can do is throw it at someone.

To take my mind off the rain and the impossible nature of my situation, I catalog all the things I hate about my current existence, starting with the wretched uniform and ending with everyone at Redwood.

When I walk in the door, I'm not at my best. "My

goodness," says Great-Aunt Irma. "You look a mess." She's wrapped in a fuzzy blanket in her recliner, pounding away on her laptop while Zeus sits on her shoulder nibbling bits of kale.

Without removing my wet clothes, I crumple in a heap on the couch. My emotions jump from being elated my father is alive to freaking out about saving him, to being furious at Jin and, alternatively, wondering if maybe Jin has a point. I try to keep my expression neutral, but the way Irma scrutinizes me, I don't think I'm doing a very good job. Lipstick's warning is fresh in my thoughts. *Consequences.* I need to distract Irma and fast.

"I had a bad day," I say. "I mean, parts of it were really good, but other parts, boy, they were awful."

Irma smiles. "Big feelings," she says.

"Big feelings!" Zeus repeats. With the kale finished, he begins chewing Irma's hair.

"Big feelings are what being a teenager is all about," Irma explains. "When your dad was your age, he was like Colorado. If you don't like the weather, just wait five minutes. You feel really good one moment and really bad the next and there is usually no reason for the swing. It's an emotional roller coaster and your job is to just hang on. Does that make sense?"

It does. But in this case, she is completely wrong. My feelings are attached to very real, very terrible reasons.

"And you've had an especially rough go." Irma leans in close. "We know you are doing the best you can."

I think she's sniffing me, probably to see if I smell like an art museum or an airport. I have to get out of here before I inadvertently blurt out everything. "You know what, I feel better having had this chat. But I have a ton of homework that I should start. What's for dinner? Can we have burgers? And those curly fries?"

Irma leans back in her chair. She's not completely satisfied with this conversation, but she's willing to let it slide. At least my bright pink cast is intact. "Yes. Burgers and fries. You got it. Go do your homework."

I try to bounce a little going up the stairs to convince Irma that I'm perfectly happy and everything is fine, but it's not easy as the enormity of my task settles in along with a healthy dose of panic. I don't even know where to *start*. If Jin were still helping me, maybe we could hash it out, work it through, throw out ideas and break them down and maybe eventually come up with a plan.

But the reality is that I'm alone and I should stop whining and just get on with it. It's not like I don't know how to be alone. I've had a lot of practice. I need to break down the problem. Obviously, the Shadow thinks Dad found the stone and hid it. When they couldn't shake its location out of Dad, they turned to me, believing that he not only told me but that I could get my hands on it pretty easily. Okay. Great. So *where* is it?

I change into sweatpants and a hoodie and climb into bed. It's easier to think under the covers. I got this. *Come on, stone. Where are you?*

I make a list of possibilities. A locker at the airport. A duffel bag stashed in a basement. A shoebox hidden in the public library. This exercise is not boosting my confidence. I pull out the red notebook and fan through it. I reread the torn pages. Did he leave me a clue? Is the answer somehow right in front of me? I review my possibilities list. I consider crying. I toss out that idea as a waste of time. I start over and go through every last thing again. This is a dead end.

I slide behind my desk. Frank is laid out, bits of him here and there. I think better when I'm tinkering. I set to work. Forty-five minutes later, Frank is looking much better, but I still have no idea where the stone is.

I am very close to despair when the cell phone on my desk chirps to life. EmoJabber flashes for attention. Jin! Probably he's just dumping me from the STEM fair team. Whatever. I don't really want to look, but at least it is a distraction from the hopelessness of finding the stone.

Jin:

EmoJabber is worse than ancient hieroglyphics. A quick assessment indicates that Jin is probably not dumping me from the STEM fair team. Unless I am somehow interpreting the rainbow incorrectly?

Me: ! ?

Jin: ! ?

Me: ?

Jin:

The lightbulb and the thinking face must mean he has an idea. But what's with the unicorn and rainbows? This is so much harder than it needs to be. How do I say "what is your idea"? And how do I say "I'm sorry for yelling earlier"?

Me: 💡 🤔 ?

Jin:

He's coming to my house? He's coming to my house and he's having a party? He's coming to my house and he's excited like it's a party? Help! Okay, get a grip, Lola! I need to figure out if he wants a burger and fries.

Me: 🍔 🍟 ● 🥬 ?

Jin: 👍 ● 🥬 🧀

I'm not sure, but I think this means he wants lettuce,

tomato, and cheese on his burger? What I do know is I feel lighter, as if a great weight has been lifted from my shoulders. But that doesn't make sense because I'm no closer to finding the stone than I was five minutes ago.

When Jin arrives, Zeus is thrilled to see him. He flutters right to his shoulder and sets in nibbling his ear.

"He only ever chews my ear," Irma proclaims. "This is a very interesting development."

"It tickles." Jin's shoulder twitches beneath Zeus's bird feet.

"Zeus," I command, "get off."

"No, he's fine."

"French fries!" yells Zeus.

We have to eat burgers before we can escape to my room and discuss Jin's idea, and it's plain torture although the burgers are excellent and the fries make me swoon. Great-Aunt Irma even sprang for these mini deep-fried apple pies, which makes her my most favorite person in the world right now. Anything seems doable with pie.

Zeus refuses to get off Jin's shoulder. He squawks and complains as Jin paces my small room, about to fill me in on his idea.

"Wait a minute," I interrupt. "I'm sorry I yelled at you before. It was not right. And I didn't mean it."

Jin waves me off. "Paul yelled at me all the time. No big deal."

"But I'm not Paul."

Jin's eyes flash and I swear I see relief. "I *know* you're not. Now, do you want to hear my plan or what?"

I nod. "Go ahead."

"I have it all figured out. First, we find the stone. Next, we access its power. Third, we use that power against the Shadow and get your father back."

There are many problems with this idea, starting with we don't know where the stone is and ending with we don't know where the stone is.

But Jin's not done. "There's more. If we can't access the power and control the Shadow, we just give him the stone and get your dad back because if the stone is not magical, there is no risk in him having it. Win-win!"

"We don't know where it *is*," I say flatly.

"Details. We just ate French fries and pie. It's the perfect time to brainstorm possibilities. Quit worrying."

The deeper we get into this mess, the more Jin's confidence grows. I'm a little envious because right now failure feels like a runaway freight train barreling down the track, intent on squashing us flat. Jin takes the pad of paper from my desk and settles into the chair, ready to figure out where the stone is hidden. "I was thinking on the way over here. If the stone chooses you, what is the first thing you would do with the power?"

"Huh?"

"What would you *do*? I'd convince my teachers to give me As so I could just stay at home and play *Fortnite* all day every day. I'd brainwash my parents so they thought I was doing something healthy like reading and eating carrots. That would be *totally* cool. Or maybe I'd make myself captain of the fencing team and win the state championships? That would also be cool. And duh, I'd win the STEM fair! Every year! Forever! Or at least until I graduate from Redwood. So what would you do?"

There are a lot of questions right now that are hard to answer—where the stone is, for example—but not this one.

"I'd get my father back," I reply.

CHAPTER 22

THE HANNAH PROBLEM

OVER PANCAKES THE NEXT MORNING, JIN AND I continue to throw out ideas about perfect stone-hiding places. He says under a tree. I say in a bank vault. He says in a pile of regular old rocks. I say this whole exercise is pointless and swipe one of his pancakes. He says I need to focus and get my own pancakes.

This is when Hannah shows up, plopping her breakfast tray down with a loud thud. Between Lipstick and the Shadow and the ticking clock and the missing stone, I forgot all about Hannah. But she did not forget about us. And she still has that incriminating video. Begrudgingly, I give her credit. She wanted something and she went for it with no apologies. I understand that. It's why I'm wearing a cast on my arm.

"Good morning, teammates." Hannah offers us a dazzling smile.

Jin glares at me. "This is on you," he says. Doesn't he realize I was just trying to protect him from getting kicked out of school or worse? And besides, yesterday I was all about kidnapping albino penguins. How was I to know that today we'd be on an actual quest for the Stone of Istenanya? I can't see the future. Jin should cut me some slack. But his expression indicates I should expect that slack sometime around the next century. Or never.

"Good morning, Hannah," I grumble.

She takes a big slurp of orange juice and wipes her mouth on the back of her sleeve. "I figure that when we find the stone and it talks to me—because of *course* it's going to talk to me—I'm going to make things happen, starting with beating old Mr. Ghetti at chess. Boy, that would make his head explode. And the STEM fair? Well, that's a given."

Jin snorts. "No way that stone is talking to you. I mean, come *on*."

"What? You think a magic rock is going to want to mind-meld with you? Your brain is like oatmeal. No way."

"And your brain is Swiss cheese. All those empty holes!"

"Takes one to know one."

"That doesn't even make any sense."

I put my head down on my arms and close my eyes. Neither of them pauses long enough to consider that Ördög cursed the stone, making its magic dark and ugly. They are both so sure the Stone of Istenanya will choose them and it will be *Fortnite* and chess wins for all eternity. They are drawn to the idea of magic despite the danger. I still refuse to believe that the stone is anything more than a rock, but I make a mental note to keep an eye on them, just in case. Power can tilt the minds of regular old people in weird directions. You just have to study history to know that.

Jin pats me on the head. "Don't worry, Lola," he says. "It will all work out."

"Have you guys located it yet?" Hannah asks, returning to her breakfast with gusto. I shove my plate aside, appetite gone.

"No." Jin spears one of my abandoned sausages. "But we were making progress until you interrupted us."

"No, you weren't."

Jin turns to me, eyes pleading. "Can we kick her out?"

"Just try it," Hannah snaps.

I drum my fingers on the table, remembering what Jin said about two brains being better than one. Which means that, logically, three are better than two. As of this morning, our two brains have not come up with anything approaching a possible location for the stone. If we had all the time in the world, we could work through the problem. But we don't. And if we are stuck with Hannah, we might as well put her brainpower to work. "Fine," I say. "Where is the stone?"

Without missing a beat, she says, "Your father talks about mailing the notebook home. Did he mail it to your house?"

"My aunt's house," I say. "She put all of his stuff in a storage locker. That's where we found it." There were rats there. I shiver at the memory.

"Oh, I remember *that* morning. So?"

"So what?" Jin says. "The storage unit was full of junk. Candlesticks. Old books. A box of rocks, even."

At the same moment, we turn to each other, mouths agape. Talk about rocks. I feel like one just fell out of the sky and conked me on the head. Of *course*! My father probably *mailed* the stone home, just like he did with the notebook, to get it as far away from the Shadow as possible, protected by the anonymity of international snail mail. And Irma tossed it in with the mosaic patio rocks. My lips flap in the breeze.

How did we miss this one? The only reason I can think of is that we were one brain short.

CHAPTER 23

A THREE-BRAIN TEAM

HANNAH TAKES A MOMENT TO GLOAT. "YOU GUYS *need* me."

"We do not," Jin replies, but less sharp now and more sheepish. We cannot deny that she saw what was right in front of us.

"Fine," I admit. "Maybe we *do* need you a little, but we don't have time for that debate right now." We have to call Lipstick before school starts and get to that storage unit, rats or not.

"I don't think we need her even a little," Jin complains, still prickly but not willing to push it. Following the path from the cafeteria into a small grove of coastal redwoods, complete with benches so students may sit and contemplate the universe or at least what's for lunch, we huddle around Jin's phone and make the call to Lipstick.

She picks up on the second ring and her personality sparkles as much as ever. "You're cutting it awfully close," she growls.

"We still have twenty hours!"

"Don't argue, kid. Exchange is set for tomorrow, Pier Fifteen, in front of the science museum. There's a statue of an atom. You know it?"

"I know it," I reply.

"Two thirty."

Is she kidding? That's right in the middle of social studies with Mr. Kind. If I miss that class, I'll be reciting the Constitution of the United States after school in detention until I grow old and die. "That's not going to work," I counter.

"Excuse me?"

"I have social studies. My teacher is mean."

"Tell me you're joking." No way. Mr. Kind is no joke.

Grumbling with annoyance, Lipstick says, "Stand by." Pier 15 is on the crowded Embarcadero, a walkway along the city's eastern shoreline, chock-full of waterfront attractions. You can catch a ferry to Alcatraz, visit with sea lions, or maybe have a meal with a view of the Bay Bridge. I guess a hostage exchange in a place overrun by tourists is normal. But what do I know? Either way, I can't miss social studies.

Lipstick offers five o'clock as an alternative. Hannah objects, citing a conflict with choir practice. Lipstick, exasperated, asks how many schedules we need to accommodate. I tell Hannah she can go to practice if she wants, that we can handle it, and she says forget that. I accept the five-o'clock hostage/stone exchange meeting. I even go so far as to thank Lipstick, who is an accomplice to the kidnapping of my father, for being flexible. Before we hang up, Lipstick issues a warning.

"Don't try anything funny," she says. Believe me, there is nothing funny about this situation. In fact, my mouth is dry and I keep gagging on my tongue. My stomach flips over on itself, like a ballet dancer on a sheet of ice. I just want to get my father and be done.

We bide our time until the end of the school day, after which we make a mad dash directly to Bay Area Mini Storage. Unfortunately, the mini storage has had a makeover, most likely in response to our last visit. New security cameras are positioned along the perimeter every ten feet. An extra layer of razor wire sits atop the fence, and the hole we cut the last time has been mended.

Which is a problem. I don't even have my wire cutters, as breaking and entering wasn't originally on today's schedule. Inside the security-guard shed, there are shadows, thrown off by the wide-awake security guard. We stand back and silently appraise the situation. The stone is so close. I can see the backside of unit seventeen from here. I give the fence a kick. It doesn't move.

"Any ideas?" Jin asks. Silence. We stare at the fence some more, waiting for a solution to present itself. It does not. Hannah is unusually quiet. Are we going to need *four* brains to figure this out?

"What if we launch you over the fence?" Jin suggests finally.

"Like a *missile*?" I ask.

"Yeah."

"Seriously?"

"You'd have to be careful not to get shredded to ribbons by the razor wire, but otherwise it might work."

Hannah giggles. I don't think I've ever heard her laugh before. "Lola the missile," she says. "I like it. In fact, I like all of this. I had no idea it would be so *fun*."

Jin and I exchange a glance. Fun is a pool party on a hot day with unlimited ice cream and soda. Being impaled on a razor wire–topped fence is not. But maybe if you never had any fun, you might be confused about the difference. Hannah's eyes sparkle with excitement.

"I am no missile," I say.

"We could pile up all our textbooks and climb over." Jin looks thoughtful. "Maybe throw a sweater over the sharp stuff at the top. No? Okay. Let me think. Do we have a pair of scissors? A pogo stick? A trampoline?"

"A blowtorch?" Hannah suggests. "Or a drone? A ladder?"

"Don't you think if we had a ladder we'd have used it already?" I ask dryly. "These are not good ideas."

Jin folds his arms defensively against his chest. "Do you have a better one?"

"Walking up to the security guard and asking politely to enter is a better idea than turning me into a human missile."

Jin lights up. "That's it! It's so simple! We just walk right in."

"I'm going to need details," I say impatiently. We are so close to the stone. It's right over this fence. It's infuriating not to be able to just march in there and get it. However, that is exactly what Jin wants us to do.

"You say you're Irma Benko," Jin says. "Your aunt never leaves the house, so there is no way anyone down here has ever seen her. We fake him out."

"But he's going to ask for identification," I counter. "You can't just let any old person into the place. That's his entire job."

"You'll just have to make something up," Jin says, blowing off my concerns. "Say you use an age-defying cleanser made with panda tears. Or, I don't know, you just have really good genes."

"It's not the worst idea I've ever heard," Hannah says. "But you're going to really have to play the part to make it work. Are you up to that?"

They must believe I am because before I know it, they shove me toward the guard's shed. I've never even been in a school play! Oh boy. All I have to do is channel my inner Irma. Be Irma. Be Irma. Be Irma. Imagining Zeus on my shoulder, I slap on a big grin and rap lightly on the window where cars wanting access are meant to pull up and talk to the guard. From the shadows, the guard emerges and I'd say he looks pleased to see me except that would be a big fat lie.

CHAPTER 24

EVEN THE TOUGHEST ROLL OVER FOR DORITOS.

THE GUARD WEARS A WRINKLED UNIFORM, WITH a smear of orange cheese-puff dust down the front. His frown indicates we have gotten between him and his snack and he is not happy. Sliding the window open, he grunts a greeting. Or I think it's a greeting. Probably he is telling us to bug off.

"Hello," I say, swallowing hard. "My name is Irma Benko. I rent unit seventeen. I'm going in to see my locker." I attempt to project confidence, as if I'm meant to be here, as if I have done this a thousand times.

The guard gives me a once-over. "What did you say your name was?"

"Irma Benko," I repeat. He's not buying it. The jig is up. We're busted. No one will show up at the meeting with Lipstick and even more terrible things will happen to my father. A bead of sweat rolls from my eyebrow. But the guard just wants to get back to his cheese puffs. He grabs a clipboard and flips a few pages, murmuring Irma's name so he doesn't forget it.

"Here we go," he says finally. "Yeah. Number seventeen. Repossessed for lack of payment. Yesterday, in fact. Your stuff is gone."

"Excuse me?" Hannah asks.

"No pay, no storage."

You have got to be kidding me. This cannot be happening. The stuff is *gone*?

"You were warned," the guard says bluntly. "There were letters and phone calls. After which we clear out the contents, sell it, and rent the unit to someone who actually pays. It's in the contract you signed."

This news makes me dizzy. I might fall over. The guard slams his little window shut, dismissing us. The last expedition I went on with my father before he disappeared, we were searching for a priceless tiara that belonged to a Russian princess who had been murdered more than one hundred years ago. There were exactly no clues as to its whereabouts, but that didn't stop Dad from visiting every living person who had a connection with the dead princess.

"It doesn't hurt to ask," Dad said. He didn't find the tiara. But that is not the point here. I bang hard on the small window with my fist. The guard returns. It's possible he is less happy to see us this time. He licks his orange fingers and glares.

"Can you tell me who bought the items from storage unit number seventeen?" I ask politely.

"No," he says. But before he can close the window, I block it with my cast and give him my best steely eyed glare. I tried it once on Irma and she wondered if I had sand stuck in my eye. The guard barely seems to register my glare at all. However, I'm not done.

"I'll give you a bag of Doritos if you answer my question," I say. The guard pauses. I've got his attention.

Jin elbows me in the ribs. "Ah, Lola? We don't have any Doritos."

"Hannah does. Right, Hannah?" Her shock almost makes this all worthwhile. I hold out my hand. She rummages through her backpack, muttering about how I could possibly know she has Doritos. The guard watches, eyes sharp with suspicion, as the wheels turn in his head. His cheese puffs are probably gone. He can't leave the booth until the end of his shift, which is possibly hours away.

"Cool Ranch?" he asks.

"Original," I say. Hannah slaps a bag into my palm. I dangle it in front of the guard. He caves immediately. It's like shooting fish in a barrel. But when he stretches out a hand toward the chips, I pull them out of reach.

"Details first," I demand. The guard, grumbling, trundles off to the computer glowing in the back of the shed. A moment later he returns with a slip of paper. I hand over the bag. He slams the window. Transaction complete.

"Merlin's Marvelous Collectibles," I read. "Water Street. Oakland."

"Merlin?" Jin asks. "Isn't he a wizard or something? A sorcerer *and* a magic rock. Doesn't the world seem so much more interesting knowing all this? I mean, magic is *real*."

Hannah's eyes have gone all sparkly again. "A wizard would be cool."

Great. This is just what we need. A wizard. "It's just a *name*," I say. "There's no such thing as magic."

"I'm going to mind-meld with the stone and play *Fortnite forever*," Jin says dreamily.

"There is no mind-melding," I bark.

"How do you *know*?" Hannah asks.

"I already told you. There is no such thing as magic." If

there were, I would order up a flying taxi or a magic carpet or a pony or something because in the real world, the one without magic, we need to get to Merlin's Marvelous Collectibles in Oakland right away.

So how exactly do we do that?

CHAPTER 25

MERLIN'S MARVELOUS COLLECTIBLES

OAKLAND IS ACROSS THE SAN FRANCISCO BAY FROM where we are and swimming is right out of the question. The water is freezing. There are sharks. And cargo ships the size of small islands. Instead, we catch a bus that drops us at the train, which takes us to Oakland, where we walk. It takes time and Jin and Hannah fill it by bickering about what they will do with magical stone powers once they get them.

I pull up the collar of my horrible uniform shirt and try to hide or, at the very least, pretend I don't know them. Ignoring my dysfunctional teammates, I think about how scared my father must be, kidnapped by a lunatic. Is he cold? Alone? Hungry? Does he think anyone is coming to help him? Since Star and Fish unexpectedly entered my life, I've not let myself go to this dark place, the one where I wonder how Dad is. It just makes me unravel. I'm much better off if I focus on the *where* of it and keep plowing forward.

Swallowing a few times, I shake off the fear and think about what we have to do next. The fog settles in and the daylight recedes as we make our way down Water Street to Merlin's Marvelous Collectibles. The property is adjacent to the Port of Oakland, one of the busiest ports in the United States. One of my favorite things to do in San Francisco is watch the massive cargo ships slip under the Bay Bridge into the port. Next to these huge vessels, the regular-size sailboats and ferryboats resemble corks bobbing in the water. Several giant container cranes loom large, like the AT-AT Walkers from *Star Wars*. I keep expecting them to break free from their foundations and destroy San Francisco across the bay.

Merlin's Marvelous Collectibles is a dilapidated warehouse, barely standing. A stiff breeze and the whole thing could end up in the ocean. The old warehouses to either side have been wiped clean, shiny new construction rising in their place. We take a moment to stare at the building. It's hard to imagine anything marvelous stashed away in this dusty old place. More likely it overflows with piles of unloved, discarded junk. I deflate. How are we going to find one little stone in all this?

An old man in raggedy, grease-stained overalls, using a cane for balance, comes out of the building. He wears a blue work shirt with the name "Merlin" embroidered over his chest pocket. Distracted and muttering to himself, he practically walks right into us.

"Oh," he says, surprised. "People. Buying? Selling? It's almost closing time."

His bright green eyes sparkle like those of a much younger man, and his long beard is expertly braided through with gold ribbon. It's a startling combination. But as Irma likes to say, we have one of everybody out here. I clear my throat. "Actually, we're looking for something. It's probably in the junk . . . ah . . . I mean stuff you just bought from Bay Area Mini Storage, that place down in the Marina?"

Merlin snorts. "One person's junk is another person's treasure," he says. My father would disagree. He believes treasure is only treasure because we all agree it has value. Junk, on the other hand, is just junk.

"Can we buy stuff back?" Hannah asks, cutting to the chase.

"Lost something important, did you?" Merlin gazes at us intently, and I get the distinct feeling he is taking our measure.

"Sort of," I say.

"That's how people usually end up at my door." Merlin grins. His teeth are too big for his mouth and very white. "Something is lost. Or missing. Or just not right. And they think old Merlin can help."

"Can you?" Jin asks.

Merlin pauses, studying Jin. Jin begins to squirm. "Sometimes," Merlin says finally. "And other times it's too late. More often than not, they want what they want but they don't know *why*. Do you understand?" We glance at each other. Nope. Not at all. Merlin taps his watch. "It's almost five o'clock. I guess that gives us a few minutes to sort you out. What do you seek, my fine young friends?" Using his cane for balance, he totters back toward the entrance to the building. We dutifully follow.

Inside, the warehouse is enormous but weirdly empty. Where are all the marvelous collectibles? Damp and mold permeate the air. It makes me gag. Hannah crinkles up her nose. Jin covers his mouth with his sleeve.

Merlin slips behind a makeshift desk, made from a plywood slab balanced on two sawhorses. "Been here forever," he explains. "But just sold out. *Everyone* wants the land under my warehouse so they can build something new, like they are doing next door. It's easy to be dazzled by fresh and shiny." He tosses a handful of papers up in the air, where they drift around him like snow. "I'm headed to Florida, yes I am. Want an ocean I can swim in without freezing my butt off. Bay Area Mini Storage, you said?" Merlin digs through the piles of invoices, finally holding up a yellow sheet triumphantly. A little burst of adrenaline surges through me and I bounce on my toes.

"Let's see," he mutters, scanning the document. "I bought one ton of material from them just the other day, probably my very last purchase, not that we are feeling nostalgic. Anyway, that means . . . yup . . . okay."

"What?" Hannah shouts, unable to contain herself a moment longer. We edge closer to Merlin. Come on! Tell us! Is the stone *here*?

"This is how it works, kids," Merlin says. "I buy junk, as you so kindly call it, by the pound and I sell it by the pound. If I buy it for less than I sell it for, I make some dough and keep the lights on. The buyers come from all over the world. They load the stuff on cargo ships and away it goes. The newest ship is called the *Nebula*, hailing from Brazil." Merlin gives a low appreciative whistle. "She's a real beauty, the *Nebula*, sleek and lean, how a ship should be. Anyhow, they load up the *Nebula* and off it all goes. I don't know what they do with it once it leaves here, but at that point it is no longer my business, so there you go."

I narrow my gaze. "Are you saying our magic rock is headed to *Brazil*?" I have spun some awful scenarios since we started looking for the stone. In my mind, I've lost it any number of ways. But not once did it go to Brazil on a big boat. Jin lays a hand on my shoulder as if to keep me from rocketing through the roof, fueled by pure frustration.

"Magic rock, you say?" Merlin's bright eyes dance. "A little on the green side?"

"It might be."

Merlin taps his nose with one of his long fingers, thinking. "I might have seen it, this rock of yours. In fact, I might have given it to Captain Silva of the *Nebula*. He seemed quite taken with it. Yes. I believe he called it beautiful. He said it called out to him, metaphorically speaking."

My heart leaps. All is not lost. "Captain Silva of the *Nebula* has our stone?" Merlin nods thoughtfully. "Yes. I am quite sure. It's a special rock, is it?"

"It *called* out to him?" Hannah has gone a shade pale. "Did you hear that, Lola?"

I ignore her. "So all we do is find this Captain Silva and ask for it back. No big deal."

"Well, it's a little more complicated than that, I'm afraid." Merlin's smile fades. "The *Nebula* sailed earlier today."

Okay. I take it back. All *is* actually lost. The stone is on its way to South America. Game over. Trying hard to hide my disappointment as it is not Merlin's fault, I thank him for his time. As we are leaving, he pulls me aside, his expression concerned. "Lola. If you happen upon this stone you seek, remember to stay true to yourself. Do not let it sway you, no matter what it offers in return."

"Huh?" I never told him my name.

"You heard me." Marvelous Merlin points a long finger at me. "Don't forget. Go on now, missy. I have work to do. Good luck. See you later. Adios."

What was *that* all about? Whatever. I don't have time to unravel it. We have a grave situation. Outside, Jin and Hannah sit on a couple of abandoned barrels. Jin's face sags. Hannah sighs aggressively. Things did not go as expected and now we need an entirely new plan. But first, a few minutes of wallowing in our misery is certainly in order.

"We tried." Jin slumps on his barrel, about to slide off.

"We *failed*," Hannah says. "On the other hand, I think it's clear that the stone is magic. Don't you agree?"

"No," I say bluntly. "The captain was using a *metaphor*."

"Metaphor or not, now what?" Jin asks.

"Maybe we substitute a fake stone for the real one," Hannah suggests. "No one has ever seen the real stone, have they, other than Captain Silva and he's way gone."

My old book of fairy tales showed Istenanya with a green sparkly stone. But that's just one illustration. There are certainly no photographs of the stone as it is not supposed to exist. Using a fake stone means double-crossing the Shadow. That sounds risky. And possibly stupid.

We sit with our new reality for a few moments, thinking about fake rocks, until Hannah jumps to her feet, upsetting her barrel. "You guys, *look*."

Out on the foggy bay, a massive freighter, heavy with cargo and riding low in the water, leaves port, gliding smoothly toward the Pacific Ocean and on to destinations unknown. "Wait a second." Jin grabs my arm. Behind the moving freighter is another ship, now revealed, gleaming in the dim sunlight.

The *Nebula*.

CHAPTER 26

STARBOARD OR PORT? BEATS ME.

THE NEBULA IS STILL IN HARBOR. IT HASN'T SAILED yet! We jump to our feet, overturning the barrels and sending them rolling toward the edge of the dock. "Our ship!" Hannah shouts.

"Hang on, *Nebula*!" I yell. "We're coming!"

"We are? We are!" Jin pumps his fist in the air. "Um . . . how exactly?"

We dash to the water's edge. Tied to the pier are a number of small fishing boats. I point to a particularly decrepit one that doesn't look exactly seaworthy. "In that."

"Are we stealing it?" Hannah asks, eyes wide.

"Borrowing," I explain. Once we liberate the stone, I

have every intention of using the same boat to get back to land.

We lower ourselves into the old boat. It doesn't seem likely to survive a large wave, but it has oars, and being as no one leaves their engine keys just lying around and I don't know how to drive a boat even if I did have keys, it's our only option for getting out to the *Nebula*. Jin and Hannah insist on rowing duty. This does not go well. Positioning themselves on either side of the boat, they row the small fishing craft like an awkward canoe, sending us in loopy circles.

"I'm going to throw up," I say.

"Jin! Just row straight!"

"I am rowing straight! You row straight!"

"You're rowing to the right!"

"No, you are!"

After a minute of this, we are a mere three feet from where we started and I fire them both. "Sit down," I command, snatching Jin's oar. They take up positions on the torn vinyl seat cushions, backs to each other, arms crossed defensively. Great. Let's hope they don't mutiny. But to mutiny, you need agreement, and these two can't agree on the color of the sky. Which is now decidedly gray. The fog thickens.

I try not to fall in the water as I crawl to the bow of the boat, clutching my slippery oar. On my knees, I paddle the fishing boat forward, three strokes on this side, three strokes on the other, no small thing when wearing a cast. The soupy air makes it hard to tell if we're making progress. It's just as likely that we are going in a circle as we are going forward. How annoyed will I be if we end up missing the *Nebula* entirely and drifting all the way to Hawaii?

"Buoy to port!" Jin yells, startling me so much I almost pitch forward into the bay.

"Which way is port?" I howl back.

"Left!" Before I can react, our little boat crashes right into a giant red shipping-lane buoy. We spin hopelessly around. Hannah grabs the second oar and fends off. The *Nebula* drifts in and out of view as the wind whips the fog. In the past eight months I've done some stupid things. However, none had such a high potential for drowning. Emily would not approve of my choices.

"Lola! Starboard!" If port is left, starboard must be right. And there is definitely something there. To be exact, the prow of an enormous cargo ship bearing down fast, like a great mythical beast emerging from a cloud, intent on devouring us.

"Paddle!" I scream. Hannah jumps onto a seat and plunges her oar into the water. Jin leans over the edge of the boat and frantically uses his hands. The ship looms closer, quietly closing the distance. "Faster!" Sweat streams down my face. We tried, Dad! We really did. But then we got run over by a cargo ship.

"Paddle port! I mean, starboard!" Our only chance is a surge of speed. The ship is upon us. We're doomed. It's over. But as the giant hull displaces the surrounding water, we get flushed away in its wake, riding a giant curling wave just like a surfer. A really bad surfer. We surge forward and rock violently side to side. I tumble back on my butt, barely able to hold on. Hannah disappears behind a row of seats. The massive ship moves by.

A moment later, Hannah's head pops up. "Are we alive? Did we make it?"

I get on my hands and knees and look around. We are not actively sinking, so that's good, but something is missing. Oh no. Jin! "Where's Jin?" Panic blooms in my chest. The water roils around us. "Jin? Jin!"

Hannah scrambles to her feet. Frantic, we scan the water around us, calling his name, but visibility is poor. What have I done? My vision narrows and I steady myself on the edge of the boat. Hannah shouts Jin's name, but her voice sounds far away.

"Jin!" I yell. "Say something!"

"We are so dead if he's dead," Hannah mutters, slapping the water with her oar.

"Not helpful," I bark.

"You are trouble, Lola Benko. I knew the minute I saw you."

I turn on her. "Then *what* are you doing here?"

"That is a very good question," she says. "I'm a smart person. I should know better. Our futures are over. We're accessories to murder."

I really want to throw her overboard, but a tiny voice draws my attention. "Help. Over here!"

Jin! Off the port bow. Or the starboard. Whatever. Without really thinking, I pull off my shoes, ditch the ugly cardigan, and hurl myself into the water.

"Your cast!" Hannah yells.

Oh, *shoot*. The heavy pink plaster fills immediately with freezing water, like an anchor around my wrist. The shock of cold pushes the air from my lungs. I gasp and dog-paddle to stay afloat. My limbs slowly go numb.

"Help!"

I swim toward the voice. "Keep talking! I can't see you."

"About what?"

"I don't care!" I gurgle, my mouth filling with salty water.

"Is port left or right?" Huh? He's quizzing me during my sea rescue? "Well, what is it?"

Swimming isn't easy with the cast, but I move forward the best I can, fighting the slush quickly forming in my brain. "Right," I say.

"Wrong," Jin says. "You're hopeless." Are we really having this conversation? Finally, Jin's pale face appears before me. He bobs in the water, clutching a tattered orange life vest, teeth chattering. "Lola, your cast."

"I thought you were drowning."

"Safety first." He gestures to the life vest. "But I might freeze to death. No wonder Merlin is going to Florida. No one freezes to death in that ocean. Lola, where's the boat?"

"Hannah!" We howl in unison, not even pretending to hide our desperation. By the time the creaky old boat emerges, I can't feel any of my body parts. Hannah hauls us up over the side and we flop into the boat like giant frozen human fish. In the cargo hold, there are several oil-stained stinky towels. We huddle under them while admiring each other's blue lips and shaking.

But suddenly Jin tosses the towels aside and jumps to his feet, pointing. "The *Nebula*!"

And there it is, our ship, looming large off the . . . ahem . . . starboard bow.

CHAPTER 27

DID YOU HEAR THAT?

CONTAINER SHIPS NEED ONLY A HANDFUL OF CREW members to operate, which is good because not only are we trespassing, but we are probably breaking a dozen international maritime laws too. The fewer people around to catch us, the better. Our footsteps echo on the steel deck. Bits of plaster cast peel off in my wake. How am I going to explain another ruined cast to Irma and Emily? I already used the exploding-volcano excuse. The shipping containers, stacked five high, tower above us like steel mountains. I jump at every shadow.

"I've calculated the odds," Hannah says flatly, glancing around. "And our chances of finding one tiny stone in all of *this* are exactly zero." A container ship can be thirteen hundred feet long. That's like the Empire State Building if it were floating on its side. There are probably close to eighteen thousand shipping containers on board, each packed full of stuff. The *Nebula* makes Merlin's warehouse look like a shoebox.

"Normally, I'd say Hannah is a pessimist and wrong," Jin adds. "But looking around . . ." He holds his hands up in defeat. "Maybe if the stone were programmed with GPS coordinates or something. Or broadcast a radio signal. Or it could just, you know, yell for us."

"In the journal, Professor Benko says the stone calls out to its intended master," Hannah says. "It finds you. Kind of like when your phone is searching for a Wi-Fi network and then, out of nowhere, service!"

"Maybe you clear your mind like meditation and, BAM, there it is?" Jin suggests.

My team has obviously lost their minds. "There are *no* talking rocks," I say. The only way we find it is by actually looking for it. And while we are standing around here debating meditation and mysterious psychic connections, the clock is ticking.

"Let's just try it," Jin implores, glancing desperately at the container mountains. "We have nothing to lose."

Except valuable minutes. But fine, if it helps Jin focus on actual searching, I'm willing to give it a go. We stand in a tight circle and close our eyes.

"Do we hold hands?" Jin asks.

"This is not a séance," Hannah snaps. "And yuck."

"Whatever."

"If you two don't stop it," I growl, "I'm pushing you both overboard. Now be quiet, hurry up, and meditate so we can get it over with."

I close my eyes. Meditation is about calming your mind, staying fully in the present, whatever that means. But shutting off my brain is no easy thing. It's a mess in there. Images of my favorite places in the world, of Irma and Zeus, of school. There's music, too, and the sound of ocean waves. And oh look, there's my dad, wondering how my mission to find the stone and rescue him has gone so far off base. I don't have an answer, so I shove him aside. Jin pops into my head next and thinking about how I almost lost him in the water makes my knees go a little weak. Okay. Push that aside. Way too uncomfortable. Now Hannah. What *about* Hannah? But my attempt at concentrating is blown when something brushes my ear, like lips whispering a secret, like a butterfly tangled in my hair.

Captain Silva.

Wait. Who said that? I swat at the air. A bug? Some sort of ocean creature picked up while rescuing Jin? But there's nothing there. I open my eyes. The fog is thick. Jin and Hannah are shimmery silver outlines. My eyes fly open, but weren't they *already* open? What did I hear? Oh, never mind. Jin and Hannah crystallize before me.

"Anything?" Jin asks. "You know, like, a stone calling out for rescue, that kind of thing?"

"Nothing," says Hannah, clearly disappointed the stone didn't jump at the opportunity to connect with her. "This is hopeless."

I glance around at the mountains of cargo containers. There's a thought in my head, something important, but I can't grab it. It's lost in the fog like Jin was. What is it?

"How do we even look?" Jin asks glumly. "The cargo containers are all locked." He's right, of course. Sealed up and secure and intended to stay that way until they reach their final destination.

Come on, brain! What *is* it? Oh! There it is! "Captain Silva!" I yell. Jin and Hannah startle. "Sorry. Marvelous Merlin said Captain Silva liked the stone. Which means he probably took it for himself. Which means it's probably in his cabin or office. Right?"

Hannah raises an eyebrow. "That's not a bad idea."

"It's as good a place to start as any," Jin adds.

The *Nebula*'s living quarters are easy enough to find, a narrow, six-story structure sprouting from the deck amid a garden of cargo, but twice voices send us scurrying behind steel containers to hide. Any second now the crew is sure to catch us. And out on the water, that probably means we walk the plank.

Once we're inside the living quarters, the corridors all look the same, white-walled and narrow. Finally, we push open a steel door to what we hope are the captain's rooms. There's a large sitting room, with a couch and a few chairs. A tidy bedroom is visible just beyond. To the right is a table stacked with magazines, and on the magazines is a gray rock the size of a tennis ball. It's not very pretty. It's kind of boring. Can this possibly be *it*? I remember it being less gray and less boring.

Except it's not really gray and boring, is it? When I turn my head just a little, the rock shimmers with a kaleidoscope of colors. When I turn back, it goes flat. I try again. Same effect. I take a few steps toward it.

"Do you guys see that?" I whisper.

"It's like a glitter bomb." Hannah's face lights up. "It's so beautiful. It *sparkles*." Everything else in the room fades away.

Jin leans into me, as if to steady himself. "It makes my eyeballs hurt," he says, flinching. I shiver, the air heavy. It's as if a ghost is breathing in my ear. My shoulders hunch up as I try to shake off the sensation.

Jin covers his eyes with his palms. "I can't look anymore. It's freaking me out."

I have said all along that the Stone of Istenanya is a rock and that's it. But what if it's *not*? What if those things the elders told my dad are true? What if Jin and Hannah are right and there *is* magic in this world? My skin chills at the thought. Either way, I have no doubt in my mind that this is the stone we're seeking.

CHAPTER 28

ESCAPING THE NEBULA

FOOTSTEPS IN THE HALLWAY RIP OUR ATTENTION from the stone. We need to get out of here. I lunge for the stone and stuff it deep in the pocket of my still-damp plaid skirt, where it is not likely to fall out. Hannah's eyes swirl around in her head. Great. I give her a shove. "Wake up!"

"Huh?"

"People coming," I hiss.

"What happened?" she asks, as if she were not in the room for the last three minutes.

Jin shakes his head, clearing the cobwebs. "I feel like I *went* somewhere." His forehead wrinkles. "But I didn't, right? I was here the whole time?" I'd love to debate the specifics of what just happened, but we are about to get busted. I shove a dazed Jin and Hannah into the bedroom closet and pull the door snugly closed. Jin's elbow is up my nose and I have a knee in Hannah's spine. Plus, it smells like feet in here.

"Don't even breathe," I warn. Through the slats in the closet door I can see a crew member, a young man with a goatee and a walkie-talkie. He keys the walkie-talkie. "Stowaway check complete. Clear to set sail."

Set *sail*? Uh-oh. A horn blasts. The floor beneath our feet begins to vibrate. Somewhere below, huge engines rumble to life, growling with effort. The ship is *moving*.

Hannah's fingernails dig into my thigh, expressing exactly how she feels about this situation. I get it. I don't want to be a stowaway to South America either. When the man with the goatee leaves, we tumble out of the closet in a heap.

"We need to get off this boat," I say.

"You *think*?" shoots Hannah. We backtrack down the narrow corridor as quickly and quietly as we can. Finally, we spill onto the deck, winding back through the mountains of shipping containers to the railing. Below, the water moves rapidly by. The horn sounds again, much louder out here. Seriously. Sailing to another hemisphere right now is just not an option.

"The ladder!" Hannah shouts, pointing. If we go down the cargo net ladder we used to climb up here in the first place, theoretically we should end up back at our little boat. The ladder has been pulled up and stowed for the journey and it takes all six of our hands, minus one, to heave it over the side. Scrambling over the edge, we descend, the three of us spread out like flies caught in a spiderweb, clinging for our lives. The ship cuts fast through the water now, gaining momentum. I can't see our little boat. Of course, I didn't use a fancy clove hitch or figure eight knot when I hitched it to the *Nebula*. No, I tied it like a shoelace. It would never hold at this speed.

"Slow down, *Nebula*!" I yell into the wind. In my mind's eye I see how this precarious situation plays out. Jin, Hannah, and I are discovered as castaways halfway to Brazil. We create some massive international incident. Emily freaks out. We miss the meeting with Lipstick. I lose my father again. The fingers sticking out of my soggy cast drift to my pocket and wrap around the stone. It feels warm, like it might be glowing. Again, I feel the strange sensation of something faint and soft at my ear, like a bug tangled in my hair.

But suddenly the boat lurches, the engines belching

and grinding. The force of the stop pulls me loose from the dangling cargo net ladder. In a panic, I grab for the net and somehow end up dangling by one foot, upside down. My horrible skirt bunches up around my waist, exposing the shorts I always wear underneath it.

Well, *now* what?

This is another two-handed job, but if I use the casted hand to help right myself, I'll drop the stone. The blood rushes to my head. Jin is down at water level already, Hannah just above him. I kick my foot, trying to free it from the tangle. I don't relish a plunge into the ocean from this height, but probably I'll make it?

"Lola!" Jin stares up at me from below.

"I'm okay!" I'm not, clearly, but this is very embarrassing.

"Yeah! Sure you are!" Hannah shouts as she begins to climb back up the cargo net ladder. I will never live this down. The ship's engines rev back to life. Hannah picks up her pace. When she reaches me, she wears a sly grin. "Nice shorts."

"I could get myself out," I protest. "But I don't want to drop the stone."

"Whatever you say."

"And I only have one good hand!"

"Yup." Working quickly, she untangles my foot and holds me tightly as I right myself. The ship picks up speed.

"We need to jump, like, now!" Jin hollers from below. He's right. But we're kind of high. No, we're really high. My mouth goes dry as a bone.

"Now or never," Hannah says. She grabs ahold of my cast and pulls me off the cargo net. She did not! Yes, she did. We sail through the air for what feels like much too long, Hannah whooping with delight the entire time. We hit the water with a splash five feet from Jin. Oh, it's so cold. Breaking the surface, we both gasp for air.

"Move!" Hannah commands. We swim rapidly away from the ship's hull, clearing a current that wants to suck us under, Hannah dragging me in her wake. The *Nebula* speeds forward, disappearing into the fog.

Of course, we are not exactly *safe*. We're in the middle of the bay, in the freezing water, in the fog, with no boat. My pink cast disintegrates before my eyes. But at least I have the stone, heavy in my pocket. I struggle to keep my head above water. I wonder if there are sharks around? Oh, now why would I go and think that? Now I see dorsal fins everywhere, all headed straight for me. A late lunch of girl in uniform. Delicious.

"Don't freak out about sharks," Hannah gurgles, as if reading my mind. "If you want to freak out, do it about ships. We are much more likely to get run over than to be eaten."

"Or we'll die of exposure," Jin adds. Aren't we just a jolly bunch! I can't imagine how much Hannah and Jin hate me right now for getting them into this. I'd hate me. In truth, I *do* hate me.

"What really stinks," Jin continues, "is we have a magic stone and we are *still* going to die out here."

"It's the wrong kind of magic," Hannah points out. "What we need is that *Star Trek* thing, where you can just beam your body places, like out of the water."

"That would be a good magic to have," Jin agrees. "But we'd need someone to do the beaming. And pretty much no one knows we're here."

"True," says Hannah thoughtfully.

We are likely going to drown. I'm about to apologize for getting them into this when something bumps me. Sharks! I knew it! This is the end! I paddle frantically, my cast splashing up bits of plaster and water into my face. But why are these two grinning? Do they hate me so much they *want* me to be torn to bits by sharks right in front of them?

"Boat!" Jin croaks. If I had to choose between getting run over by a boat or eaten by a shark, I think I'd take the boat. But it looks like I'm going to get both because I am *just* that lucky.

"Lola, behind you." I spin to discover our creaky little boat, floating just over my shoulder. I have never been so happy in my life and I'm including the time I got a private tour of King Tut's tomb, which was all sorts of amazing. We hoist ourselves, bedraggled and breathless, into the boat and collapse in a heap on its dirty bottom.

"Are you guys okay?" I ask, but my lips are frozen and the words sound funny.

"Who cares about that?" Hannah gasps. "You still have it?"

Oh yeah. I hold up the stone triumphantly. It glimmers despite the fact that there is no sunlight, only gray.

"We're a good team," Jin says.

"We are," agrees Hannah.

And it's true. Last week we were three people alone, but now we're a team, at least for right now. In a minute we will have to get up and start paddling, but for now we lie in the bottom of the boat, shoulder to shoulder, and relish our unexpected success.

CHAPTER 29

WHEN IN DOUBT, BLAME THE SPRINKLERS.

GREAT-AUNT IRMA IS MAD AT ME FOR NOT REPORTING in on my whereabouts earlier. "It's dinnertime! Remember I gave you a phone so I could call you. I had no idea where you were! It was highly upsetting."

I apologize all over myself and promise not to be late again, but honestly, this is exactly the reason I don't carry the phone. I could just see her pinpointing my location and finding me in the middle of the bay. How exactly would I explain that? But that's not the worst of it. She's also highly skeptical of my sprinkler malfunction story. "If a sprinkler malfunction destroyed your cast," she asks, "why do you smell of ocean?"

"It was a geyser of water," I explain. "*Everything* got wet. And you know Redwood is practically on the bay. The whole place stinks like salt. I just absorbed the smell."

"Stink!" Zeus screeches. He lofts from Irma's shoulder to mine and begins to peck furiously at my hair. After a moment, he triumphantly produces a piece of seaweed, waving it around in his sharp little beak. Traitor! See if I ever give you any more kale bits.

"Grass," I say preemptively.

Great-Aunt Irma narrows her gaze. "Did you go somewhere you were not supposed to be?"

"No." Yes.

"Did you take anything that didn't belong to you?"

"No." Well, not exactly. The stone was in the captain's possession, but that doesn't really count. Dad had it first, so, by proxy, it kind of belongs to me. Right?

"Okay, then," Irma says. "You're going to have to blow-dry that cast before it totally falls off. And take a shower. It's like *20,000 Leagues Under the Sea* in here."

Zeus finds this hilarious and starts squawking, accidentally swallowing the seaweed. Serves him right, the little brat. Gagging, he upchucks it into Irma's hair. Gross! Irma grabs him. "Naughty bird! Keep it up and I will pluck you like a chicken!"

"Chicken! Chicken!"

Grateful to be forgotten among the chaos, I dash for the shower. As the hot water washes away the chill, I think about how we giggled all the way home from Oakland, reliving the highlights of our adventure and absorbing serious side-eye from rush-hour passengers as we dripped puddles on the train. It was like we were in a bubble, our own world, and I found myself wondering if this is what having real friends felt like. But I shouldn't get ahead of myself, right? We're just on a mission together, a quest—me, to find my father; Jin, because he made a deal; and Hannah, to make sure we don't win the STEM fair by magical means. We are not exactly friends.

It takes me over an hour to blow-dry my cast. Next time I'll get a waterproof cast.

According to Jin's plan, we need to see if the stone is really magic, so the following day we agree to meet after school with the stone and the notebook and test it out. If it works, we can use the magic on the Shadow and free my father, and if it doesn't, we hand it over and get him back anyway. Win-win, as Jin said.

Despite the experience in the captain's quarters, with the stone shimmering and glimmering and showing off, I'm still skeptical. Sure, it's pretty, but so is a cherry tree in bloom or a perfect rose. And pretty is not magic.

I intended to hide the stone in my locker, but after what we went through to get it, I'm feeling weirdly protective. I don't really want to let it out of my sight. It remains in my pocket, banging against my thigh with every step I take. I spend social studies daydreaming about the reunion I will have with my father. It seems so close now I can almost reach out and grab it. I have so much to tell him! About my bedroom at Irma's, my new school, Jin and Hannah. When Mr. Kind calls on me and I don't know the answer or even the question, he moves straight to humiliation.

"Miss Benko," he says, his sharp eyes studying me. "Why don't you share your thoughts on last night's reading?"

I did read the material. I swear I did. But it was hard to concentrate with the stone sitting on my desk. I was mostly staring at it, waiting for it to perform some magic and at the same time knowing how crazy that was. But nothing happened and it got late and I had to go to bed. In short, I have no memory of what the reading was about.

"It was . . . um . . . historical," I mutter. The stone glows warm against my thigh. My fingers graze it, as if for comfort or maybe strength when dealing with the exceptionally nasty Mr. Kind.

"Brilliant," he says. The class snickers. "Tell us more.

Spare no details. We want a glimpse into that cesspool of a head."

Oh, I wish he'd shut up! Go harass someone else! Can't you see I'm dealing with a lot of stuff right now?

Suddenly, Mr. Kind begins absentmindedly patting his pockets for the glasses lodged on his head. "On second thought," he says. "Andrew, please read section 28.2 aloud. Pay attention now, class. This is important."

My fingers wrap around the stone. Andrew reads, my transgression all but forgotten. When the bell finally rings, I flee to my locker. Hannah is already there, bouncing on the balls of her feet. Jin is next, flicking his bangs repeatedly. They are anxious. And excited.

"That cast has seen better days." Jin smirks. "Ready?"

"As I'll ever be." *Let's get this done. The clock is ticking.* We head to the Redwood library, bypassing the doughnuts because we don't have a lot of time. I clutch the stone, the notebook tucked securely in my backpack. I'm jumpy, sure Lipstick is going to leap out from behind a tree and snatch our precious cargo.

Finally, tucked into the rainbow beanbags, I place the stone on the floor in the center of our tight circle. I pull out the notebook and read.

"'The village elders speak of how the stone chooses a

person and whispers to them. It feels like a shiver, as if a spirit is floating nearby. The stone calls out to you, quiet but persistent. At first it makes you feel good, powerful, but soon you are overwhelmed and willingly perpetrate great evil on its behalf.'"

Silence settles over us. Dad's words feel much heavier now that we have the stone. "I don't know if this is a good idea," I whisper. I know I agreed to Jin's plan to try to access the stone's power, but are we just asking for trouble?

"We can handle it," Jin responds, waving me off. He's completely focused on the stone, determined even. So is Hannah. There is no turning back.

"Okay then. Here we go. We are supposed to feel its presence. Everyone try."

We close our eyes and concentrate, just as we did on the *Nebula*. But on the ship the stone was far away and now it's right here. Jin fidgets beside me. I can hear Hannah's steady breathing. A decent interval passes. "Anything?"

Jin shakes his head. "Crickets." Hannah agrees. Nothing. This is starting to feel silly.

"It *has* to work." Jin frowns. "We almost drowned trying to save it. It owes us. Do you hear that, stone? You *owe* us."

"Maybe it wanted to go to Brazil?" I suggest.

"Oh," Jin replies. "I didn't think about that. Maybe

the reason it's not doing anything is because it's mad we screwed up its travel plans."

"I was joking," I say flatly.

"Let's try one more time," Hannah interrupts. "Really concentrate this time. Like no thinking about *Fortnite* or doughnuts or homework or anything. Just think about the stone." I can't be sure if Jin doesn't think just a little about *Fortnite*, but it doesn't matter. Nothing changes. We stare at the stone. Hannah gives it a little kick.

"Come on," she whines. "Do something, you stupid thing." But insulting the stone's pride doesn't motivate it to burst out in magic, spreading fairy dust and unicorns all over the place.

Turns out, at the end of the day, it's just a rock.

CHAPTER 30

DOUBLE CROSS

OUR REACTIONS ARE, NOT SURPRISINGLY, ALL OVER the place. "I was so sure it would work," Jin says, crestfallen. His entire body sags with disappointment. He really *believed*.

On the other hand, Hannah is just angry. "We almost died," she says with a huff. "I want a refund."

"This is the worst day ever," Jin complains.

But the truth is, I'm relieved. I have what the Shadow wants. I can hand over the stone without worrying about potential world-ending consequences and get my father back. Magic, while undeniably cool, really would just complicate things. I glance at my watch. It's time to head to the Embarcadero.

But before we go, I make an offer. "You guys have done enough. I can do this part by myself. If you want out. I mean, I almost got you killed and stuff." Jin needed help with winning the STEM fair and Hannah didn't want Jin to get a leg up with a magic stone, but now we're talking about actual bad guys. Things have changed. But even as my exit offer hangs in the air, I hate the idea of going it alone.

Without missing a beat, Jin shakes his head. "We had a deal. You help me. I help you. I'm not going back on a deal."

"And I don't have anything better to do," Hannah says with a shrug. "I might as well come along and see what kind of mess you get into next. You'll probably need rescuing at some point anyway."

I hide my smile behind a hand, faking a yawn. "Then we'd better get going."

As we race to the bus stop outside school, Hannah wonders aloud if the real Shadow will actually appear and if he does, will he be transparent, like an actual shadow? Jin says that's ridiculous, but that does not stop them from arguing about it for ten minutes. The bus stop is crowded with kids ready for the weekend. Conversations float around about meet-ups and hangouts. Someone asks if there is a better puke emoji than the regular one with the green vomit.

A lengthy conversation ensues over the value of purple puke. What does it *mean*? Hannah and Jin have strong opinions, but all I can think about is the Embarcadero. My palms are glossy with sweat. Am I a bus ride away from finally seeing my father again? Is this nightmare almost over? I could be back to my regular life in a couple of weeks, on the road hunting treasures with my dad. This should fill me with excitement, but right now, watching a bunch of Redwood kids argue about which color puke means what, I feel a pang of regret. Or something? Go away, you stupid confused feeling! I need to focus.

When the bus finally drops us at the Embarcadero, we make our way through the throngs of tourists to Pier 15, home of probably the best science museum ever. It has all sorts of hands-on experiments with electricity and it's hard not to love a museum that encourages guests to semi-electrocute themselves in the pursuit of knowledge. We have twenty minutes to kill until five o'clock, but that's not enough time to go inside. Outside the museum's entryway is the metallic sculpture of an atom. Standing off to one side, I scan the crowd, my heart banging hard against my ribs. What if no one comes? What if this is all a setup? What if the Shadow never had my father to begin with? Why am I thinking this *now*? We stand in silence and watch the tourists stream by. The minutes feel like hours.

"Lola Benko, how nice to see you again." But here is Lipstick. Right on time. Today's lip color is a shade of bright orange that should never be applied to one's face on purpose. Lipstick grins, revealing a smudge of orange on her sharp incisors. She could be a vampire with those teeth. That would certainly complicate things.

"Stop staring," she says defensively.

"Not staring." I cast my eyes down at my shoes. Lipstick stands too close and I catch a whiff of something citrusy and harsh, like moldy oranges.

"Do you have the stone?" Her eyes are alive with anticipation and she licks her lips hungrily, like she plans on eating it or something.

"I do," I squeak.

"Show me," she commands.

"Where's Professor Benko?" Hannah steps in front of me, arms crossed. "No way we hand over that stone until we see him."

"I'd ask who *you* are," snaps Lipstick, "but I get the feeling that we'd be here all day." She speaks into her watch. "Bring him over."

Two men emerge from a crowd. One is short and wiry, with black hair buzzed close to his scalp. The other wears a plaid shirt that barely holds back his belly. Between Buzz and Plaid is a man. I can't see his face, but I'd know that ratty leather jacket anywhere. My *father*.

"Here he is," says Buzz.

"The brilliant *professor*," adds Plaid, his voice dripping with disdain.

My knees buckle. Jin grabs me just before I collapse. Hannah rushes to help. Dad is too skinny and his face is gray and drawn. When our eyes meet, he smiles weakly. I want to run to him, but Lipstick sets me straight. "Don't take a step in that direction until you hand over the stone."

I dig it out of my backpack. A cluster of people blocks my view of Dad. Lipstick's eyes lock on to the stone as I place it in her outstretched hand. She practically drools. It's not very dignified.

"Let him go," I croak, my stomach tightening like a fist. "You have the stone."

As Lipstick's long fingers close around the stone, she grins. Not a nice-doing-business-with-you grin but more of an evil power-hungry grin. It's just a rock. There is nothing to worry about. I haven't done anything wrong except free my father. "Silly little girl." Lipstick's frosty tone gives me an instant ice-cream headache. "I thought kids today were smart. Well, here's the deal. There's been a change of plans. The Shadow needs your father for a wee bit longer. He's the one who knows all the stone's secrets. Otherwise, it's just an expensive paperweight."

I am trying to process what she's saying, but my brain is arguing that it cannot be true. I brought her what she wanted! "You promised," I bleat, just as pathetic as can be.

"Are you double-crossing us?" Jin asks.

"I knew it!" Hannah yells.

"Look how quickly you catch on! Bravo!" My skin itches with tension. I want to spring on Lipstick and push her over and take back my stone, but I'm frozen. "Oh, come on. Such faces. Don't despair. If your father helps us access the power of the stone, he gets to go. The Shadow is not unreasonable. It could still work out."

This fills me with horror. The stone isn't magic, and nothing my father says or does will change that. It's like the Salem witch trials' ordeal by water. If a witch sank, she was innocent but drowned anyway. And if she floated, she was a witch and they burned her at the stake. Lose-lose. Just like this.

"It's just a rock," I whisper. "It's not magic."

"It had better be magic if he wants to live. And don't think about going to the police. Remember those consequences we talked about? They have only gotten more extreme." It's the perfect walkaway line. She tucks the stone into her pocket and gives a nod to Buzz and Plaid, who push my father in front of them, not even allowing him a glance back in my direction. And there I stand with no stone and no Dad.

How could I be so dumb?

CHAPTER 31

MY FEATHERED FRIEND

I ACT ALL NORMAL AT HOME, BUT I'M HOLLOW inside. If someone bumps me, I will likely shatter. What will happen to my father when he can't wring magic from an ordinary rock?

Irma asks me about school, but I can't remember anything beyond the Lipstick debacle. I blither about math class and pottery, and if Irma suspects anything is wrong, she doesn't let on. I barely taste the pizza we have for dinner even though it's from my favorite place, the one generous with the pepperoni. Irma tells me she spent her day on a virtual visit to the Louvre Museum in Paris. She's making a "Ten Cities in Nine Days" virtual tour app for seniors. They can travel the world and never leave their living rooms.

"I actually stood on top of Michelangelo's *David* statue," she says casually. "Right on his head! There's a whole different perspective from up there."

"I bet there is," I reply, offering what I hope looks like a genuine smile because it sure doesn't feel like one. She had a better day than I did. She didn't screw up *everything*.

But Zeus knows something is wrong. He climbs on my shoulder and chews my hair, stopping every few moments to squawk "Lola!" in my ear. He doesn't even hop off when I go upstairs. Sitting at my desk, I tinker with Frank 2.0, trying to keep the overwhelming feeling of despair at bay. What have I missed? Is there an angle that I can play? Where is *my* different perspective?

But no matter how I look at the situation, all I see is failure. "Tell me what to do," I ask Frank. Not surprisingly, he doesn't answer. The Shadow, the stone, and my father could be anywhere. I had one chance and I blew it. My eyes threaten tears.

"Poor Lola," Zeus coos. He flutters from my shoulder to my desk and pecks my knuckles.

"Ouch. Stop that!"

"Lola," he squawks, lofting into the air and out my

door. He returns with a blue hair ribbon I have never seen before. He places it before me on the desk before taking off again. This time he brings me a refrigerator magnet of the Eiffel Tower. He adds that to the ribbon.

Five minutes later I have a small pile of odds and ends gathered from around the house. The tears well up. Zeus, that stupid bird, is trying to make me feel better. He's bringing me presents. This time a slice of orange, his favorite, hangs from his beak. He plops it down in front of me. The juice leaks out. But when the citrusy scent hits my nose, a flicker of memory ignites and I almost tumble out of my chair.

Lipstick's *perfume*. Tewksbury's wedding cake mansion smelled of Lipstick's perfume! My heart begins to race. *She* was the one in the room, the one I was waiting on to leave so I could get in there and take the statue! That's why she seemed vaguely familiar.

Oh boy, if the wedding cake mansion belongs to Tewksbury, and Lipstick, who works for the Shadow, was there, that can only mean one thing: Tewksbury and the Shadow know each other! Wait a minute, it could mean something else, too. It could mean that Lipstick is using Tewksbury to help the Shadow. Or that the Shadow has something on Tewksbury and is forcing Tewksbury to help him in his quest for world domination and Lipstick is the go-between. Or Tewksbury and the Shadow are willingly working together.

In any case, there is a connection between Lipstick, Tewksbury, and the Shadow. This makes me dizzy and a little nauseous and a little excited all at the same time. Zeus watches me, busily sucking on that orange slice. He doesn't seem at all concerned about my situation.

Zeus is right! Get a grip, Lola! Think! If Tewksbury and the Shadow are accomplices, there's the very real possibility that the wedding cake mansion is where they are holding my father! I spring to my feet.

"Zeus, you're a genius!" I kiss his fluffy bird head and he makes terrible gagging noises. But I don't care because I have a new plan. Go to the wedding cake mansion. Find my father.

Without thinking, I EmoJabber Jin because he refuses any other mode of communication. It takes some back-and-forth for me to convince him to get on the phone. We can't exchange important information on EmoJabber on account of the Shadow and Tewksbury being in cahoots, but I'm not good enough with emojis to get that point across.

The moment Jin picks up, I yell, "Tewksbury and the Shadow are friends! Or maybe Tewksbury is being blackmailed? I don't know. It doesn't matter. Anyway, it was Lipstick's perfume!" I must be loud because Zeus flutters out of the room, feathers ruffled in offense.

"Who?" asks Jin. He sounds sleepy. "What? Perfume?"

"The rotten oranges. It's a unique smell. Gross, really. Trust me. And it was at the wedding cake mansion and it's what Lipstick wears."

"Who's having cake?"

"No cake. Keep up, will you?"

I explain it again and Jin is not happy about Tewksbury potentially being a bad guy. "He sponsors the STEM fair!" Jin howls. "He's *nice*."

"I'm sorry, but there is the potential he's an evil jerk."

"I don't like this scenario." Jin is forlorn. "I'd prefer blackmail."

"Sorry. But listen." When I explain the part about my father possibly being held in the wedding cake mansion, Jin says, without pause, "I'm in."

"But I didn't even tell you what we're going to do."

"Don't care. Still in. It's what real friends do. I won't let you down."

At first his response throws me and then I fill up with a fizzy, light happiness, kind of like soda bubbles. It makes me feel bigger somehow. And braver. We *are* friends.

"I can get us inside," I say, determined. Yes. That's what I'm going to do. I'm going to get into that house and find my father. I have a real friend now! And I've had just about enough of being pushed around by the Shadow and his minions.

It's time to shine some light on this situation.

CHAPTER 32

OVERKILL

THE BREAK-IN MUST BE TONIGHT. THE SHADOW IS bound to have more accomplices than just Tewksbury. He probably has access to mansions all over the globe, and if he decides to move his operation to take over the world somewhere else, there is no way we can follow him because we have no money for travel on account of me being unable to steal any art. We agree to wait until midnight and meet at the bus stop between my house and Jin's.

"Wear comfortable shoes," I say. "And bring a flashlight. No phones. I don't want to be tracked. And anything else you think we'll need."

"Like doughnuts in case we get hungry?"

"*Practical* things," I clarify. "And I'll bring Frank."

Jin pauses. I can almost hear him roll his eyes over the phone. "Didn't you just say practical things? Are you going to throw him at somebody?"

"He's ready," I say.

"He *is*?"

I stare at Frank 2.0 and the parts I have not yet put on him littering my desk. No, he's not ready. But he *has* to be. No doubt the wedding cake mansion has been wired to the hilt since my last break-in. If we so much as sneeze on a doorknob, an entire army of bad-tempered security guards will likely swoop down and cart us off to jail. But Frank is going to disrupt those cameras so they can't see us. "He can do it," I say.

"If you say so."

"Jin?"

"Lola?"

"Do we call Hannah?" She blackmailed us with that video. She stole my notebook. But I remember how she crawled back up the *Nebula* cargo net ladder and untangled me. And she pulled me into the water before I chickened out and sailed to Brazil. And without her we might never have found the stone in the first place. If I'm being honest, Hannah is the friend you want on your side if a zombie apocalypse happens. Or you need to find your lost father in the bad guy's mansion. She's not afraid. But does Jin feel the same way? There's that nemesis thing and all.

"Well," Jin says after a pause. "Maybe she's not so bad. She doesn't panic and run away from stuff. I guess she's reliable, too. Sometimes even a little funny. And you know what they say."

"I do?"

"Two brains are better than one, and three brains are better than two. I'll see you in three hours."

When I call Hannah, she acts like I just invited her to an amusement park with the world's best roller coaster. "Oh, excellent! This is the perfect opportunity for me to test out some new things I've been working on. Can't wait! This is going to be a blast! See you soon!" Does she even consider the downside of our high-risk activities? I bet not. Her eyes are probably doing that sparkle-with-excitement thing right now. When I first saw her at Redwood, sitting at a table all alone, I never would have called it. First impressions are *not* reliable.

When Irma goes to bed, I fill my backpack with every-thing I might need. Duct tape, pliers, a hammer, a length of rope, an old version of the Window Witch that lacks elegance but should get the job done. Gently, I place Frank on top of everything. One of his new googly eyes sags and his pipe-cleaner antennae are bent. He looks forlorn. I refuse to see this as a sign of what's to come.

Using the emergency rope ladder, I sneak out of the house, but it's not a clean getaway. Zeus catches me in the act and I have to bribe him with a handful of jelly beans, which are forbidden because they make him crazy. I sprint to the bus stop, where Jin and Hannah are waiting, standing in the shadows.

"Sorry I'm late." I bend over my knees, gasping. "But the bird busted me."

"I don't even want to know the details," Jin says, shaking his head.

"No. That's probably best."

"Fortunately, my mom was at the restaurant," Hannah says. "So I just strolled out the front door. No wild attack birds. She would flip out if she knew I was running around the city with friends in the middle of the night, hunting magic rocks." She snorts at the idea and Jin cracks up. But her words are ringing in my ears. *Friends*. That connection I felt after we survived the *Nebula* and found the stone glows bright. None of us is alone anymore because we are together.

After a moment, they realize I'm not laughing along, a little lost in the feeling. "Lola looks serious," Jin observes. "Like she's thinking. Or napping."

"I hope you're thinking about how we get into the wedding cake mansion," Hannah adds.

Suddenly, I'm grinning at them like a fool. We are about to do something dangerous and potentially very stupid and yet I'm bursting with happiness. It's too embarrassing to explain, so I get on with explaining what's next. "I got it all figured out. I'm a pro, remember? We climb up the wall, just like I did the last time. We turn on Frank to block all his security. We use the Window Witch to get inside. We find my father."

"Basically, what you did before, minus the falling two stories and breaking your wrist?"

"Yes." And this time I'd like to leave with what I came for.

The night bus is quiet, just a few people snoozing toward the back. I pull Frank onto my lap and tinker with his guts. There is nothing I can do now to make him work better. Mostly, I just need to keep my hands occupied so they don't shake. Hannah stares at Frank, indignant. "*That's* the electromagnetic pulse generator?"

"Function over form," I grumble. "Pretty gets you nothing."

Hannah snorts. "I can't believe I was afraid you guys were going to beat *me*. That thing is a mess! What does it even do?"

"It's going to get us into the mansion undetected," Jin says confidently. I give him a wan smile. If Frank fails, Jin and I will suffer humiliation on a level heretofore unseen in the middle school STEM fair arena. Plus, we will likely get arrested. And lose my dad. The stakes are *high*.

The bus stops and picks up a few stray passengers. "Whatever." Hannah shrugs. "You guys and your Frank. Well, take a look at what *I* brought along." She opens her backpack and pulls out two tin lunch boxes.

"Doughnuts?" Jin asks hopefully.

"Don't be a dope." Hannah flips open the lunch boxes to reveal their contents. One holds a small plastic device, about the size of a deck of cards, that looks like a modified transistor radio from the 1970s, but way cooler. A small button glows blue at its center. A coiled pair of headphones is tucked in beside it. The second lunch box contains a pair of thick boxy goggles.

"I couldn't decide between a hearing amplifier and night vision goggles for STEM fair," she says smugly. "So I'm proto-typing both." *Two* projects? There are no random wires hanging out of either, or charred plastic. "Constructed completely from stuff you might find in your garage or kitchen. I'm dying to test them."

Hannah, aspiring spy or thief? Could go either way.

CHAPTER 33

THIS WAS UNEXPECTED

THE WEDDING CAKE MANSION IS DARK AND ominous, but only because I know that inside is a madman who kidnapped my father and is busy plotting world domination. Otherwise, it would just be dark.

Jin is salty, mumbling about Hannah and the definition of overkill and why she feels like she has to do two projects when a normal human would only do one. I'm more concerned that Frank will explode the minute we turn him on. While I've made vast improvements, I would not venture so far as to call him reliable just yet. We stand on the sidewalk trying to look casual and doing a poor job of it. Jin hops from foot to foot and Hannah chews her cuticles like she has them to spare.

A man walks a pint-size dog on the opposite side of the street, his face illuminated by the blue glow of his phone. We wait for him to pass before squeezing through a gap in the hedges and into the yard. The little hairs on my arms prickle. I just know Dad is in there. I can *feel* it. This is going to work!

Or maybe it won't. The ivy that is meant to be covering the wall is completely *gone*. "Is this the wall we're supposed to climb?" Hannah asks, following my gaze.

"You mentioned ivy," Jin adds.

"We have a problem," I whisper. Murdering the ivy was the obvious thing to do in response to my break-in, even if it was not so nice for the ivy. I should have anticipated this. When I came here for the ballerinas, I planned everything down to the tiniest detail. This time I thought about it for ten minutes. Dad likes to say that when the going gets tough, the tough get going. A difficult situation is just something to work through. Get comfortable being uncomfortable. And the missing ivy sure makes me uncomfortable. I scan the side of the house for a different way in that will not get us immediately caught. The wall is smooth and whitewashed, not even a protruding brick to use as a hand-hold. There are no windows on the first floor, and the second story is abnormally high up because this is a mansion and everything is grander than in a regular old house.

But off to one side of the wall, the missing ivy has exposed a rusty drainage pipe, bolted every five feet, running straight up to the roof and right by a balcony, perfect for our purposes. "We'll use this," I say, giving the drainage pipe a tug, as if to prove it is stable. Which it is not. It creaks and grinds against the wall. The ivy was probably the only reason it didn't collapse.

"You're kidding, right?" Even in the darkness, I can see the fear in Jin's eyes.

"It will work. I swear."

"You go first." Hannah steps aside and gestures to the pipe. I wedge my foot on the first bolt. It's slick and it takes a few tries to secure. I have to be faster. Every second we stand around out here, we are closer to being doomed. And I don't want to be doomed. I want to get in this stupid house. I pull myself up with my one good hand, grabbing the pipe and pushing my chest forward so gravity doesn't yank me off. Wedging my knees on either side of the pipe, I press them together to create enough stability that I can reach higher. I pull up and slide my knees. It is not elegant, but slowly I begin to move toward the balcony. Five feet up, I wedge my foot in the next bolt and stand, taking a moment to catch my breath.

"How's it going?" Jin whisper-shouts.

"Oh, piece of cake."

"You're lying," Hannah says, matter-of-fact.

"I am. But I only have one hand. So please be quiet. I need to concentrate." It takes about ten minutes for me to get to the second-story balcony, where I fling myself over the edge and promptly collapse in a heap. It takes about thirty seconds for the panting to stop. Finally, I wave down to Hannah and Jin, gesturing for them to hurry up.

"No big deal," I whisper.

And for Jin it's really not. He makes it look easy. Must be his long arms and legs because he is next to me in no time at all and he's not even tired. Hannah goes next. About halfway up, she freezes. This is the girl who climbed up the *Nebula*'s cargo net ladder to save me from certain death, or at least something very unpleasant? What is she doing down there? We don't have all night. Any second now, there will be dogs or a police helicopter or something else awful. I know from experience.

"Come on!"

"It's coming off," Hannah whimpers. "The *pipe*." And

just as the words leave her lips, the pipe begins to peel away from the wall. Instinctively, I lunge for it, almost pitching clean over the balcony railing. Hannah screams. Not good. Quickly, I wedge the pipe into the crook of my good elbow. Hannah clings like a koala bear to a eucalyptus. But gravity is fighting hard to pull me down too.

As my balance falters, I envision calamity. Broken bones and Judge Gold and making license plates until I shrivel up and die. The Shadow *wins*. I can't fall. I can't let go of the pipe. Abruptly, I stop plunging.

Jin has me firmly by the belt loops. "No sudden moves," he whispers. I nod, gently so as not to disrupt our very tenuous balance. "Hannah, don't move."

"Oh, no way," she says. "Not moving. But I might pee my pants." This makes me giggle. I shouldn't giggle. Giggling will send both of us directly to the ground.

"Stop laughing," Jin commands. "Or I will let go."

I clamp my lips shut as Jin slowly reels me back from the edge. I keep a firm hold on the pipe. When Jin and I have it steady, we instruct Hannah to climb. It takes her a minute to get going. I get it. It's scary to fall two stories. Finally, Hannah tumbles onto the balcony, landing on her back, gasping and sweating. "My legs are shaking. I don't feel so good."

"I saved your life," Jin gloats. "I can't wait to remind you the next time you're being a brat."

"You're the worst," she says, breathing rapidly. "But thanks for not letting me fall to my death anyway."

An awkward silence follows. "Um, you're welcome?"

I give her another minute to recover before urging my team on. "Getting up here was only the first step. We haven't even gotten to camp three yet."

"Who said anything about camping?" Jin asks.

"*Everest* camp three," I explain. "It's the third place you stop when you're climbing the mountain, when the hard part is still in front of you and you basically can't breathe. In other words, we have a lot to do."

"You sound like your dad," Hannah says.

Jin agrees. "I mean, I've never met him, but that's the kind of thing I imagine him saying."

Dad would have anticipated the ivy problem. Dad would have seen the double cross coming. Dad would never have turned over the stone in the first place, no matter what. He would have had a proper plan. Me, I'm just making stuff up as I go.

Hunkered down on the balcony, I pull Frank out of Jin's backpack. Hannah's right that he is kind of a mess, but I love him anyway. I fix his pipe cleaners to give him some dignity. "Frank," I say, in all seriousness. "You cannot mess this up. You have to do what you were meant to do. Shine, little guy." Jin swallows a few times but doesn't say anything. Hannah rolls her eyes. "Ready?"

Jin nods. His hands shake. I flip the switch. Frank glows. Frank hums. My shoulders tense, waiting for him to blow, but miraculously he doesn't. Settling into a low hum, he radiates a soothing blue light, hopefully scrambling all the video surveillance and computers in the house.

"Frank is good to go," I say after a minute.

"You think?" Jin is barely breathing.

"Eighty-five percent sure." Actually, more like eighty-two. But they don't need to know that.

"As long as you don't cross the purple and yellow wires, we're good," Jin says.

"What happens when that happens?" Hannah asks.

There's a pause. "Stuff," Jin says finally.

"Here we go," I say. It's the moment of truth. I grasp the door handle. Gently, I pull it open, waiting for a screaming alarm.

But nothing happens. I open the door a little more and still there is no sound but the hum of our machine and the din of faraway traffic. I look at Jin and grin. "He *works*."

"Wait a minute," Hannah whispers. "You weren't *sure*?"

Jin high-fives me and dances around in a circle. I grab his jacket just as he is about to twirl off the balcony. When we enter the dark interior of the mansion, the floor creaks ominously beneath our feet. Hannah pulls out the night vision goggles and slips them on. She looks like a walrus.

"Follow me," she says. And we do.

CHAPTER 34

A KNIGHT IN SHINING ARMOR

I'M HIT BY PUNGENT ORANGE, A HARSHER VERSION of what I smelled the first time I was here. Does Lipstick just walk around spraying her perfume like air freshener? This room is bigger than the one where I found the ballerinas. It's a grand office, just the kind I'd envision an evil tech mogul having. Or a king. And there are cameras *everywhere*. Ones that look like giant fish eyes on the ceiling, ones fixed and bolted to the wall, and others that pivot and scan. Boy, Tewksbury sure is paranoid, but I guess I can't blame him. After all, this is the second time I'm creeping into his mansion uninvited. I say a silent prayer that Frank is up for the job.

The office is paneled in dark wood. Large paintings, vivid with color, line the walls. On one side is a desk the size of a small car. In the middle of the room, two crimson sofas face each other and behind one is a console table bearing a sculpture of two silver balls welded together to resemble a decapitated snowman. Very modern. Probably expensive. And much less likely to stab me in the butt.

"Don't even think about it," Jin warns. He's right. After I rescue my father, art theft will no longer be necessary. Figures. Just when I was getting good at it. Well, not really. Hannah pulls out her hearing amplifier and taps the little blue light. The weird device glows in the darkness.

"Won't Frank mess it up?" Jin asks.

"It's on a radio frequency," Hannah says, plugging in the headphones. "Totally basic and totally fabulous. It's so sensitive that I can hear people *breathing*." Holding it up, she waves it around looking for a signal. She turns a dial. She mutters to herself.

"No people close by," she announces. "Come on."

We pass out of the office, leaving behind all that valuable and easy-to-steal art, into a dark hallway. Hannah leads the way and we follow on padded feet, trying for complete silence. But as we turn the corner, we plow right into a tall shadowy figure. Naturally, Hannah screams and throws up her arms. But it's *not* a person. It's a suit of medieval armor that explodes with a spectacular crash. Metal parts rain down on us. The voice amplifier in Hannah's hand erupts with gruff, surprised shouts of alarm, loud enough we hear them through the headphones. We need to get out of here. And fast.

"Go back," I whisper. Scrambling out from under a heavy helmet and other bits of armor, we charge to the office and throw ourselves behind the sofa, under the table with the headless snowman. We are folded together like a puzzle. My nose is in Hannah's armpit. Gross.

"This is bad," Jin mutters. "This is *so* bad. We broke a *knight*."

"Be quiet," I hiss. Jin clamps his lips together. I can't see her clearly, but I think Hannah might faint. That would also be bad.

I recognize the voices. They belong to Plaid and Buzz, the two burly men we saw at the Embarcadero. We don't need an amplifier to hear them in the hallway. They flick on the lights to find armor scattered all over the place. Obviously, this is cause for concern.

"The dog?" Buzz asks.

"Nah," Plaid responds. "He's down in the kitchen with our guest."

"You make it sound like we're running a luxury hotel here or something. Maybe it was the wind that knocked it over?"

"Like, someone farted and blew out the armor?"

Snort. Laugh. "Not that kind of wind, you idiot."

"Oh, *outside* wind. I get it. But the windows are closed."

"Maybe the rats did it?"

Did he just say *rats*? A little shiver runs up my spine. We have enough going on, hiding out from these two. I can do without rats.

"They're getting bad, aren't they? Fancy house like this, you'd think they'd do something about them. Maybe send in the dog?"

"That little thing? They are twice his size."

Giant rats? Well, that's just great.

There's a pause. We don't move a muscle. This is much harder than it sounds, considering we are tucked in here like sardines.

"Wish Jones would get those security cameras back online," says Buzz. "It's creepy up here." He sneezes. "And dusty. Well, let's have a look around anyway. Not getting paid to stand around and do nothing." I experience a little thrill. Frank is working!

They throw on the office lights. This is it, the end. I set

my jaw, determined to get captured with some dignity. Not that dignity is easy with an armpit in my face. Images of Buzz and Plaid are reflected in the glass of the French doors. We could definitely outrun Plaid, but Buzz might give us problems. He looks mean. Plus, there is nowhere to run.

But lucky for us, Plaid and Buzz are not very good at their jobs. They glance around the living room while discussing what kind of lattes Buzz should bring back on his upcoming break. They settle on vanilla soy, extra hot. They never even *enter* the office. Turning off the lights, they disappear the way they came, leaving the armor in a heap. "They don't pay me enough to clean up medieval messes," Buzz says with a sniff.

Under the table, we collectively exhale. "That was *close*," Hannah whispers, wiping sweat from her forehead.

It was. And while I was a little fixated on the idea of giant rats, I also heard them say they had a "*guest*." They have to mean my father.

"Your dad must be in the kitchen," Jin says.

"And the cameras are still down," Hannah points out. "Frank may look like a demented bunny, but he works."

Jin glows in the praise. "Pretty cool, right?" While Frank still shields us in a cloak of invisibility, we have to find the kitchen. And fast.

CHAPTER 35

UNDERGROUND

WE PROCEED WITH AN ABUNDANCE OF CAUTION, ON account of randomly placed knights and giant rats. The amplifier doesn't pick up any noise of human activity, so it's safe to assume Plaid and Buzz are busy drinking lattes and not lying in wait around the next corner.

Using the night vision goggles, Hannah guides us down the long dark hallway to another wing of the house. There are bedrooms and a home gym and a door leading to a narrow set of stairs. These would have been used by the servants a hundred years ago when this house was built. Servant stairs usually lead right to the kitchen. Silently, we nod at each other and creep down the stairs. We are stealthy, invisible, concealed in the shadows. And there are no rats, so, by my measure, everything is going pretty well.

And that's usually when I should get nervous.

At the bottom of the stairs is a corridor leading to the kitchen. The lights are on, but the amplifier is silent. I gesture for Jin and Hannah to stay put while I scope it out. Of course, they ignore me and we tiptoe closer in a tight cluster. But the kitchen is empty. No father. Sharp disappointment pokes me in the ribs.

"Maybe they meant *under* the kitchen?" Hannah whispers, pointing at a door. The basement. Not many houses in San Francisco have basements, but it seems like a great place to hide someone. We creep across the kitchen and tentatively pull open the door to reveal a rickety wooden staircase.

Hannah adjusts her night vision goggles. Between the goggles and the headphones, she looks like she's going into outer space. But space cannot be darker or more foreboding than this basement. With each step down the slatted stairs, I'm completely sure a giant rat is going to drag me away to his rat lair and devour me. To say my heart races is an understatement. It's about to bust clear through my chest.

"Lola," Jin pleads, "your fingernails." I have Jin's arm in a death grip and there is really no excuse for mauling him.

"Sorry," I mutter. We continue down the steps until we hit the concrete floor. It smells moldy and dank down here and it's cold. There is not a glimmer of light. Without Hannah's goggles we'd be in serious trouble. "Do you see anything?" I ask Hannah.

"Just boxes and old paint cans." She scans the room. "Oh wait. That's weird." She lurches forward and we stumble after her.

"What is it?" Jin hisses.

"Look." She pulls the goggles off her head and pushes them against my eyes. Everything is shades of gray and black, but I know what she's looking at. It's like a water-tight hatch on a ship, opened using one of those circular spinning handles, built into the stone wall of the basement. "Weird, right?"

"Very."

"Give me those." Jin yanks the goggles from my eyes, grabbing a handful of my hair in the process. Ouch! "Okay. I agree. Weird."

"I guess we go through the weird door?" I ask.

"Nothing else down here." Hannah shrugs. It takes all three of us to rotate the wheel and open the door. It creaks and moans and finally swings open. Hannah bravely steps through first.

"It's a tunnel." I pull out my flashlight and cover it with my palm to dim the light. She's right. A tunnel carved out of the rocky underbelly of San Francisco, heading off into darkness in both directions. An inch of dirty water covers the ground. The tunnel's ceiling is high enough that I can stand up straight but just barely, and it's about as wide as the three of us shoulder to shoulder.

"What the heck is this?" I shine the light on a rounded wall covered in cobwebs, and shiver.

"The World War Two tunnels," Jin whispers. "I've heard about these."

"But they were sealed up years ago," Hannah explains. "People were coming down here and causing all sorts of trouble."

"I think the Shadow drilled his own entrance," I say. It's brilliant. No one is *ever* going to find him down here.

"Which way?" Jin asks, pulling out his light. I have no idea. Both ways are dark, wet, and uninviting.

"That way," I reply, pointing left. Slopping through the smelly water, we trudge off down the tunnel. This would be the perfect place for giant rats to live, right? No, Lola. Do not think about the rats!

"What are we looking for exactly?" Hannah asks. I'm not sure, but I feel like we will know it when we see it.

"Just keep going," I urge. The ground is strewn with garbage and hunks of broken brick. I trip over a piece of debris and nearly take a header into the dirty water. We come to a fork in the tunnel. "Left." I try to sound confident, like I know where we are going, but it's possible we will be lost down here forever and in two hundred years some intrepid archaeologists will discover our fossilized remains and wonder why we were so stupid.

This new tunnel is darker and tighter. I'm sure there is enough oxygen down here for us. *Of course* there is. We are about fifty feet past the intersection when butterfly wings tickle my ear. But there are no butterflies down here.

You are going the wrong way. What you are looking for is in the other direction.

Huh? "Do you guys hear that?" From their expressions, the answer is clearly no. It must be an echo, some distant sound distortion due to the rocky walls. Yes. That's what it is. "Never mind. Keep going."

Hello? What's the problem? I said you are going the wrong way.

I stop dead in my tracks. "Lola? Are you okay?" Jin shines his flashlight right in my face. "You look weird."

Tell them.

"Stop that," I say, swatting the flashlight away. "I think

we need to turn around. This is the wrong direction."
Hannah steps closer, next to Jin. They study me while I
squint in the bright light.

"What do you mean?" Jin asks.

"What we're looking for is back that way." I point down
the tunnel.

They exchange a glance. "How do you know *that*?"
Jin asks.

I shake my head. It feels sticky and slow. "I don't know.
There was something in my hair. Like a bug. And then a
whisper. It said we were going the wrong way. It was probably just some weird echo thing. Sound bouncing off the
walls maybe?"

Jin and Hannah stare at each other. "No. Way." Jin
falls back a step.

"It's the stone," Hannah says, shocked. "It's talking
to *you*?"

"That's insane. Probably I'm just dehydrated."

"Say something back," Jin urges. "Quick!"

"No!"

"But what if it really is the stone trying to communicate with you?" Hannah asks. "Just try. Come on, Lola. It's
the *stone*."

Fine. To be honest, the whisper sounded pretty friendly,

if a little aggravated by my slow response. It didn't feel evil. And if I try, I will inevitably fail and they will leave me be. A win-win, like Jin is always talking about.

Ah. Hello? Stone? Are you there? Um, this is Lola calling.

We wait. Jin and Hannah eyeball me. I feel like I have spinach stuck between my front teeth. I turn my back a little, shielding my face. But there is no soft breath at my ear. No butterfly in my hair.

"It's not answering," I say. "Because the whole idea is just *insane*. And the longer we stand here, the more likely it is that we get caught."

But without argument, we turn around, passing the door we came through and heading off in the other direction. We walk in silence for a while. What if it really *was* the stone? I know it didn't sound scary, but why would I trust it? Maybe it's just using me to get out of here? Maybe it has its own agenda?

Stop it, Lola! Right now! You're just tired and hungry and you've had a lot of stress in your life. Just ask Emily. You are here to get your father. Don't forget your mission. And there is a perfectly reasonable explanation for the weird mosquito butterfly whispering in your ear. Perfectly. Reasonable. I think?

Great.

CHAPTER 36

LISTEN UP, WORLD.

IN THE DISTANCE, LIGHT FLICKERS. THERE IS something up ahead. As we draw closer, voices drift toward us. To one side is a bunker, about the size of a large bedroom and designed to shelter San Franciscans in the event of an attack during World War II. We creep closer, using the shadows for cover. The bunker has smooth concrete walls and a single bulb dangling from the ceiling, casting eerie shadows. We hunker down just short of the wide entrance, invisible.

Lipstick faces our direction. Even down here, at this point, the Shadow lets her do the dirty work. He's a terrible boss even if she is a terrible person for agreeing to work for him in the first place. She stands over a person bound to a metal folding chair. *Dad!* He slumps miserably. A lump fills my throat and tears threaten to spill. I squeeze my eyes shut and inhale through my nose.

Lipstick appears annoyed. But that might be her default expression. "Do you know that EmoJabber is worth billions of dollars? Cute, right? But when I first conceived of the idea to create a platform where emojis did the talking, no one would listen to me. No one would take my calls or listen to my pitch or invest in my idea or *anything*. I thought it must be because it wasn't a very good idea. I spent a lot of nights telling myself I was worthless."

My father's face remains neutral. What is she saying? *She* invented EmoJabber? But that's not right. Tewksbury did.

"But the idea wasn't worthless," she continues. "And neither was I. I just needed to present it differently. So I invented Benedict Tewksbury."

The little hairs on the back of my neck stand at attention. She *invented* Tewksbury? As in, Tewksbury doesn't *exist*?

"Excuse me?" my father snaps. It's the tone he uses when I do something dumb and I should know better, like not watching my feet and almost falling into a crevasse in the Himalayas. "What exactly are you saying?"

Lipstick's mouth curls into a sharp toothy grin. "You fool," she says. "*I'm* Tewksbury. *I'm* the Shadow."

Hannah elbows me hard between the ribs, wide-eyed with surprise. Jin's mouth is a perfect O of shock. I'm suddenly breathless. I considered a lot of scenarios when I realized that the Shadow and Tewksbury were connected, but no *way* I saw this one coming. They are *all* the same person and that person is *Lipstick*.

My father gasps as if someone just punched him in the gut. I know how he feels. Lipstick grins. "Bet you never thought the silly little assistant could actually be the master?" She circles my father. "How easy it was to disguise my voice, to play up the mystery of a tech genius never being seen in public! How happy everyone was to accept his backstory of fancy schools and deep connections. And did the money ever flow when they thought I was just one of the boys. The heart of gold stuff just made my invention more irresistible, STEM fairs and school scholarships and all that goody-goody stuff. People are so easily fooled. They see what they want to see."

"I don't . . . understand."

"Of course you don't! You've been played. I know all about your Task Force, trying to keep these objects all to yourselves. But here's the thing your ridiculous, greedy little team doesn't understand. You can rely only on yourself. People will let you down. Every. Single. Time."

Lipstick gazes into the distance beyond my father. Loneliness flashes in her eyes, and desperation. But there is something darker, too. Anger. After a second, she shakes it off and refocuses on my father. "Now, it's true that there's not much money can't buy, but all the people I hired to find the stone failed. Again, I needed another approach. So I flooded the networks I know you monitor with rumors that the mysterious Shadow was searching for the stone and was close to finding it. If I can invent one personality, why not another? I knew this would get you out of hibernation. The Task Force would put you on it at once. And you, of all people, might really find the stone. Which you did. Brilliant plan, eh?"

"You have so much," Dad says slowly. "I don't understand why you seek the stone."

"EmoJabber gets me into their lives," Lipstick continues, gleeful with anticipation, "and the stone gets me into their *heads*. Maybe I want a thousand-person dance mob on the Golden Gate Bridge, just for kicks, at *rush hour*. Or I want a bunch of tourists to steal the Crown Jewels on my command. I'd look fine in a crown, don't you think? How about handing over the details on what my competitors are working on? That would be a good use of the stone's power. The possibilities are endless! It's going to be heaps of fun!"

My father pulls at the ties binding him to the chair. "You don't understand what you're messing with here," he growls. "The stone is dangerous."

"Blah. Blah. Dangerous." She waves off his concern. "I learned a lesson back when I invented Tewksbury. Power is the only thing people respect. And you can never have too much. It was only a matter of time until someone found the stone. I just made sure it was *me*."

"You kidnapped me," Dad says flatly.

Lipstick shrugs. "Collateral damage. These things happen." I catch a glimpse of the stone in her hand. She casts loving glances at it. Creepy. Why not get a pet if you want something small and cute to love? A hedgehog or a kitten?

"We will have so much fun later," she says to the stone, placing it in a sturdy safe bolted in the corner. Oh no. Not a safe. I'm an amateur when it comes to breaking safes, as in I have no idea how to do it. And I have nothing in my backpack of tricks to help.

In the bunker, Lipstick crouches down in front of my father. "It's not that bad," she says. "Just think, you will witness the stone's power firsthand."

"I won't help you," my father hisses.

"Oh, but you will," Lipstick says. "If you don't want that daughter of yours meeting with misfortune. We'll get started later. In the meantime, don't go anywhere."

Cackling at her own joke, she strides toward the bunker exit, right at us. Instinctively I push Jin and Hannah flat against the wall, into the dark shadows. If we are perfectly still and pretend we are just part of the tunnel, she should walk right by us. We are underground in a system of tunnels that have been barricaded from the outside world for years. She does not expect us to be here.

We need to be one with the wall. Bricks and concrete. Please, oh please don't see us. Beside me, Jin fidgets. I find his hand and squeeze it hard to settle him down. Hannah is still as a statue. Tewksbury, aka the Shadow, cruises right by, disappearing down the dark tunnel.

But she will always be Lipstick to me.

CHAPTER 37

CAUGHT. AGAIN.

MY FATHER SAGS IN HIS CHAIR, DEFEATED. IT'S ALL I can do not to run right up to him and tell him everything will be okay even if I don't know that it will be. But Jin holds me back. "Just to make sure she doesn't come back," he says quietly.

There is so much I want to tell my father—about Jin and Hannah and the STEM fair and the Jelly and Zeus and Irma and Redwood Academy and Judge Gold and my room with the cute kitten comforter and how I'm really good in science class and I was thinking I might learn fencing. Or soccer. I might make a good goalkeeper, having nerves of steel and all. Who knows?

"Well, what do we have here?" I whirl around to find Buzz carrying a tray with a sandwich and a glass of water. My first thought is, Dad does not like tuna salad. My second thought is, uh-oh, now what?

"Are you *really* here to break out your father? How amazingly nervy and stupid you are." A walkie-talkie dangles from Buzz's belt. A flashlight is clipped there as well, swinging back and forth and casting loopy circles of light at his feet.

What I think he wants to do is hold the tray in one hand and key the walkie-talkie with the other, alerting Lipstick and Plaid to our presence. But the tray wobbles and the sandwich slides precariously to one side. Not wanting tuna salad all over his shiny black boots, he pauses briefly to steady it.

In a flash, Hannah leaps forward and conks him on the head with the flat hard side of the voice amplifier. Jin jumps in, kicking him swiftly in the back of the knees. The sandwich flies up in the air and the plate crashes to the ground. Buzz goes down in a heap, smacking his head on the concrete, out cold. The tray clatters to the ground. Jin and Hannah stand over him, grinning like superheroes who have just discovered their powers. My jaw hangs open.

"You *guys*."

Jin holds up a hand for a high five and Hannah slaps it hard. "That was amazing," Jin says. "*We're* amazing."

"I guess that makes us the muscle of this operation." Hannah flips up the collar of her jacket.

"Hey," my father calls out. "Who's there? What's going on?" And that's when I rush to him.

It takes a few minutes for me to stop simultaneously laughing, crying, and hiccuping to explain how we got here. "I've been trying to find you because I knew you weren't dead. And I stole a statue from Tewksbury who is the Shadow who is Lipstick. But I fell out the window, two stories, and wrecked it. Which is why I have this cast. And then Judge Gold sent me to Redwood instead of jail. Where I met these guys."

"Hold the phone. Jail? And you broke your *wrist*?"

"It's a long story," Jin says.

"And complicated," Hannah adds.

"And then Lipstick made a deal with us. And we found the stone on a ship going to South America and almost drowned in the bay. And then we thought we were trading it for you, but Lipstick is a double-crosser. And then we found the entrance to the tunnels in the basement of the wedding cake mansion. And . . ."

My father holds up his newly freed hands. "Let's sort

this out later, shall we? We're in a bit of a pickle at the moment." He hugs me close. The musty smell of his leather jacket threatens to start the tears all over again.

"Escaping might be a good idea," Jin suggests.

"But the stone," I say. "We can't just leave it."

"Forget about the stone, Lola," my father responds. "We'll deal with it later."

"But, Dad. There's something we need to tell you."

"It really is magic!" Jin blurts. "It talks to Lola. The stone, I mean." Dad goes a shade paler, and that's no easy thing, considering he doesn't look his best to begin with.

"It *talks* to you? Oh dear."

"It tells me things. Or I think it does? But what if we leave it and it decides to talk to Lipstick?" If Lipstick harnesses its power, an army of EmoJabbers will march across the world, leaving a wake of destruction without once using a proper word. I just can't let that happen. Plus, I've really had it with Lipstick.

Dad pats me on the head. "Look at you. Never one to back down even when the odds are against you."

The odds are *always* against me. Outside the cave, Buzz groans, starting to come around. We are running out of time. "Whatever we're going to do, we need to do it fast," Hannah says.

"Right." Dad is all business. "Does anyone know how to break into a safe? No? Me either. Thoughts?"

"Ask the stone for the combination," Jin urges me.

"I can try." I feel remarkably silly, but here we go. *Hey, Stone! Wake up! It's me! Do you want to be rescued or what?*

It takes a few seconds, but finally the butterfly whisper returns.

Took you long enough.

Just my luck. A sassy magic stone. *Quit complaining. The only way I get you out is if you give me the combination. Do you happen to know it?*

I know lots of things. 35-24-18-7.

"Thirty-five," I whisper. "Twenty-four. Eighteen. Seven." Jin drops down in front of the safe, turning the dial frantically. *Click.* It pops open. My father chokes, gasping and muttering. Jin holds up the stone triumphantly. I can't tear my eyes from it.

"Lola?" Jin asks. "Hey, Lola?"

"Okay. I'm good. Just give me a sec." I try to shake off the sensation, but it clings to me like a sticky cobweb.

"That's not it," Jin says.

In the entrance to the cave stands Buzz, wobbly but on his feet and ready to blow a gasket.

CHAPTER 38

EASY COME, EASY GO

BUZZ RUBS A BIG BUMP ON HIS FOREHEAD. "YOU knocked me out," he complains. "Nobody has ever knocked me out before."

Hannah shrugs. "Turns out I'm pretty strong." Buzz holds a can of pepper spray, finger on the trigger. My father shoves the three of us behind him and steps forward.

"I understand you're upset." Dad is calm and soothing. "But we can talk this out and reach an accommodation. I'm sure of it. I know people. I can get you out of this. At the very least, let the children go."

"These children are dangerous," Buzz says indignantly.

"The children can't help with the stone. Only I can. Keep me. Let them go."

What is he saying? And why am I just standing here? I have a magic stone!

Hey, Stone? Can you get Buzz to, you know, buzz off? Make him think he's a peacock or something. That would be funny.

I wait for the butterfly whisper, but nothing comes. Uh-oh. What did Dad say about the stone using the person and not the other way around? Or maybe the stone is napping? Or maybe it just needs to warm up to me like a cat? It's not like I have an owner's manual to consult or anything.

Stone? Please? Things are pretty bad right now.

Clearly, the stone does not care about my problems. What good is a magic stone if it doesn't work? Worthless stone! Jin and Hannah watch me. I shake my head. Forget it. Buzz strides up, bold as ever. "Hand it over."

"No way."

"Lola," my father commands, "give him the stone."

"But . . ."

"*Do* it." I put the stone into Buzz's outstretched hand, but I don't want to. I want to do like Hannah did and hit him in the head with it.

"I'm going up top and telling the boss." Buzz tosses the stone up and down like a baseball. "She's not going to be happy." Outside the bunker entrance, he hits a red button and a heavy steel door slides across the opening, locked with a heavy latch that can only be opened from the outside.

Things have definitely taken a turn for the worse.

Hannah pounds on the door with her fists. Jin gives it a swift kick. This doesn't help. We are trapped. I drop to my knees and hold my head in my heads. "I'm sorry," I say. "I lost the stone."

Dad wraps his arms around me and kisses the top of my head. "Water under the bridge," he says. "Who cares? What I want to say is that you're pretty amazing, Lola Benko. You all are!" We collectively beam at his praise. Sadly, it is short-lived. "Of course, coming after me was incredibly foolish, dangerous, and wrong on so many levels I cannot even count that high. But still, quite brave." Dad looks at us expectantly. "Now, how do we get out of this mess? Anyone happen to have a phone handy? Aren't you kids always tethered to your phones?"

"Lola said we couldn't bring them," Hannah explains. "And they aren't allowed at Redwood."

"Oh, I like this new school very much." My father lets me go. He strides to the door to study it, running his hands around the edge. His brows furrow in concentration. "If we could somehow break the latch from the inside, we might be able to slide the door open manually."

The three of us step up to have a look. "We'd need a bomb to go off to break that latch," Jin says, disheartened.

Did he just say *bomb*? "We have one of those!" I shout.

"We do?"

"Frank!" I drop my backpack to the ground and pull out Frank, still happily humming along, glowing blue.

"What is that?" Dad asks, looking a little horrified.

"Oh, that's just our STEM fair project," Jin says. "It's an electromagnetic pulse generator. Lola made it."

"She did?"

"And Hannah made the night vision goggles and the voice amplifier," he adds. "Without all three, we never would have made it this far."

"But the pulse was Jin's idea," I say quickly. "It really took both of us." I squat down by Frank and try to remember the process for making him explode. I'm sorry, Frank. You did everything we asked of you, flawlessly, and in return I'm going to ruin you. But I promise to rebuild you again, to make you better, stronger, and possibly more pretty, if you think that matters.

I dig my fingers into Frank's guts, disconnecting and rerouting the wires. Blue, green, and red wires this way, and the purple and yellow like this. "When I cross these wires," I explain, "it will take about sixty seconds for Frank to heat up and blow. And remember, once that happens, the security cameras will be back online. We don't have much time."

"I'm concerned," my father says.

"You got any other ideas?" Hannah asks.

"None," he replies.

"It will work," I say. Jin grabs the extra set of shoelaces from his backpack and helps me bind Frank to the door latch. "Ready?"

My father looks worried, but Jin and Hannah nod. "Do it," Jin says.

Quickly, I attach the wires and flee to the farthest point in the bunker from the door. We huddle together and my father drapes himself over us like a human shield. Oddly, it pleases me that he clearly believes Frank has the potential to put us in danger.

Thirty seconds. The smell of burning plastic fills the room. Forty-five seconds. Frank starts to hiss and spit sparks. And at sixty seconds, just like clockwork, he explodes. I duck my head and close my eyes. The room fills with smoke. Jin coughs.

"Gross." Hannah fans away the thick air clouding the

room. I race to the door. Frank lies in smoldering pieces and the latch is completely detached, dangling precariously by a thread.

"Brilliant," my father says, gagging just a little. "Now everyone, push!"

We place our hands flat against the steel and heave it to the right with all our strength. At first it doesn't budge. I envision Lipstick, Buzz, and Plaid charging our way. We push again, hard, and the door begins to give.

"Harder!" Jin yells. One more time and the door slides open just enough for us to slip through. Free of the cave, we run, without looking back.

CHAPTER 39

RATS

THE TUNNELS FORM A COMPLICATED LABYRINTH beneath the city. Dad wants to know why we didn't use some sort of bread-crumb system to mark our way, like Hansel and Gretel who, by the way, came really close to being eaten by a witch. I remind him that we can't go back the way we came as that is where our particular witch currently lives. I don't think she's cannibalistic like in the Hansel and Gretel story, but you never know.

"I think it's this way," Jin says at yet another tunnel intersection. "It feels right."

"Feelings are not good science," my father replies. But at the moment, feelings are all we've got. We follow Jin's lead. Is it possible that it's getting darker? Our flashlights do little to penetrate the gloom. In stealth mode, we move quickly and quietly. There has to be another way out of these tunnels that isn't sealed up. I'm hungry and tired and would like for this rescue to be over now. But it's not over. Not by a long shot.

Hannah stops abruptly in front of me. In the darkness, I bump into her. "Hey!"

"Shhh." She holds a finger to her lips. "Do you hear that?" It's a rushing sound, kind of like a river or a constant wind. It's far away but growing louder by the second.

"Oh dear," Dad says. "I think I know what is going on here. Lipstick, as you call her, mentioned she has used this tactic a few times and greatly enjoyed the effect." Tactic? What? It's close now. Whatever is causing the sound is almost upon us. "Try not to lose each other, but more important . . . run!"

I turn back to the last tunnel intersection just in time to see a wave of rats come around the corner and barrel toward us. Millions and billions and trillions of rats. It's an amazing amount, shocking, unbelievable, ridiculous, *not* okay. It's possible I immediately die at the sight of them coming toward us like a living nightmare. I'd prefer zombies. Or vampires. Or grizzly bears. Honestly, anything but rats. But the screaming that fills the tunnel is my own, drowned out by the thunder of little twitchy feet. I throw my flashlight in the air.

"Stay ahead and on top!" Dad yells. "Like an avalanche!" I have never been in an avalanche and certainly not one of rats. And they are not small rats. They are big sewer rats, fat and happy and being driven on a wild rampage by Lipstick, probably with fire or water or something they fear. I can't stop screaming. Running and screaming is not as easy as it appears in the movies. An acrobatic rat launches from the tunnel wall into my hair. Another clings to my leg. Still a third slithers across my shoulders. I can't even cry. And I definitely can't breathe. I'm hyperventilating. Any second I am going to pass out.

Oh, no way! I *cannot* fall down on the ground! I'll be buried in them! Run, Lola, run! Surf this wave of rats! I close my eyes and plow forward. Unable to see my father, Jin, or Hannah, I follow a small pinprick of light. The smell is overwhelming, a furry, damp, musty animal smell. What if we don't get out? What if the rats herd us into a dead end and just keep coming, eventually suffocating us with their numbers?

Don't think like that! Out of the darkness, a hand grabs mine. Jin. He yanks me into a small space off the tunnel, a smaller version of the bunker where Dad was held. Where are the others? Are they here? Have they been swept away? "It's okay," he murmurs. "It's okay. The rats aren't in here." I still feel them on my skin. They are everywhere. Panic rises in my throat. I can't get it to stop. I push away from Jin and flail into the wall of the little cave.

Imagine my surprise when I crash right through it, falling headfirst into darkness.

I regain consciousness to see three looks of grave concern, but none with whiskers or pointy little ears. It's dark and damp. Quickly, I check my fingers to make sure the rats didn't bite any of them off. I figure my toes are safe because my shoes are still on. There were so many rats. I didn't know there could be so *many* rats. "Lola?" Dad places a hand on my forehead as if checking for a fever. "Say something."

"Where are we?" I croak.

"You saved us," Jin says proudly. "By freaking out and falling through that wall, which led to a subway tunnel. Now we just have to walk out."

"Rats?" I whisper.

"They're gone." Dad uses his soothing voice. I must be a mess.

"I generally don't have a problem with rats," Hannah says. "They are wicked smart and some kinds make good pets. But that was . . . a lot of them." She shivers.

"Lipstick is quite creative," Dad says. "I will give her that."

I try to sit up. My head hurts. "That was the worst," I mutter. "I mean, really, I'd have taken ants or bees or spiders or anything else."

"Okay, spill it," Hannah says, hands on hips. "What did rats ever do to you?"

"I don't want to talk about it."

But Dad does. He sits down on the hard ground beside me, leaning against a wall. "When Lola was three," he begins, "I took her to Egypt on an expedition with me. Her mother had just left us, you see, and I was afraid to let Lola out of my sight."

"*Dad*. Really?"

He ignores me. "During the day, when I was working, I had a woman from town look after her. Apparently, they encountered some rats and it was very unpleasant for Lola and she has been uncomfortable around them ever since." *Uncomfortable?* I sit up.

"The babysitter left me in our tent and four rats *attacked* me," I say with a sniff. "It was not uncomfortable. It was terrifying." I remember their beady little eyes and twitchy whiskers as if it were yesterday. They were huge and clearly had a plan, spreading to the corners of the room and closing in on me from all directions. I was paralyzed with fear.

The rats bit my fingers and toes. They pulled my hair and chewed my clothing. It was like they were taunting me, laughing at my distress. Finally, I started screaming so loudly half the village came running. Needless to say, the babysitter was dismissed.

But that was when I decided that I would never let fear paralyze me again. No standing around doing nothing. Forget that. Although it's pretty clear that rats still freak me out, at least I did not freeze and let them overwhelm me. "I'm perfectly okay with all the other animals on the planet," I say defensively.

"What about scorpions?" asks Jin, smirking.

"Or poisonous snakes?" Hannah grins.

"Polar bears?"

"Oh wait. I've got it. Albino penguins!"

Jin and Hannah giggle uncontrollably, clutching their sides and high-fiving. Already I need new friends because mine are obviously defective.

"You three certainly recover from trauma quickly," my father observes. "But perhaps we should make our way out of here before we are run over by a train?"

I will not even try to explain the looks we get when we finally reach a subway platform and climb onto it. Words cannot do them justice.

CHAPTER 40

SURPRISE!

TO SAY GREAT-AUNT IRMA IS SURPRISED TO SEE US
is an understatement. She faints dead away, dropping at
our feet with a thud. Alarmed, Zeus flutters around in a
tizzy, pecking at Dad's head and shrieking. When Irma
wakes, her eyes fill with tears.

"I never thought I'd see you again," she says, hugging
my dad. "I was so sure that this time you'd gone and actually gotten yourself killed."

Dad hugs her hard. "If not for Lola and her friends, I
might not have gotten out of this."

Irma makes a pot of bitter tea and Dad tells us how the
International Task Force for the Cooperative Protection of

Entities with Questionable Provenance asks for his help from time to time finding artifacts that might possess qualities "uncommon on earth."

"He means magical, my dear." Irma pats my hand.

"Wait a minute," I demand. "There are *more* stones out there?"

"Not stones, exactly," Dad replies. "But . . . other things. Yes."

"And all these years that we've been running around the world looking for lost things, you were really on missions for the International Task Force on . . . whatever it is?"

"No, not at all," Dad says quickly. "Just . . . *sometimes*." I cannot believe this. I mean, I'm a pretty observant kid. Or I thought I was. "The ITFCPEQP is really just concerned with the safety of all involved. Entities with questionable provenance can be dangerous."

"Magical objects," Irma repeats.

I have questions. Lots of questions. What are these magical objects? Where do they come from? Why are they here? Who made them? What does the Task Force *do* with them?

"Oh," Dad says. "Most everything we hunt for turns out to be, well, ordinary and very much of this world. But once in a while there are things that are more difficult to explain. Those items we keep safe, and away from the general public. Knowledge of their existence can cause problems. As you have seen. That's all."

That's *all*? This and all his other answers are deeply unsatisfying. "I engaged in a life of crime to save you," I say pointedly. "I almost got sent up the river. You owe me a proper explanation."

Needless to say, Irma is a little dumbfounded to discover that my crime spree was simply a means to an end. "I should have seen that coming," she says thoughtfully.

"I had to finance my mission to find Dad," I explain. "Travel is not cheap."

"The important thing is that I put you in danger this time," Dad says. "I will never forgive myself."

I'd argue that while that is an important thing, it is not *the* important thing. I restate my questions: Why, where, who, and what? But Dad stands slowly, reporting that he must make immediate contact with Star and Fish and bring them up to speed so they can stop Lipstick.

"Star and Fish are quite skilled at this part," Dad says. "I feel sure the stone will be in good hands in no time at all."

I'd like to see Star and Fish again. I'd like to kick them

in the shins for acting like I was pathetic when I claimed my father was still alive. I'd like to yell at them for losing track of him, for not keeping him out of harm's way. What kind of two-bit operation are they running anyway? And they have *got* to do something about their name. All those letters!

Dad is on the phone for much too long, and eventually, Irma insists I go to bed. It sounds like the best idea ever. I'm exhausted but happy. I found my dad. I accomplished what I set out to do. There will be time later to unravel all the details, to get my questions answered, but that can wait. For the first time in eight months, I fall into a deep dreamless sleep.

When I awake suddenly, a few hours later, I have no idea what time it is or where I am. It takes me a second to recognize my room. Everything is normal. Everything is fine. Dad is here, just down the hall. He's safe. But a bug buzzes my ear. I swat at it.

You sleep like the dead.

Stone? Now?

Were you expecting someone else?

Where were you before, when we needed help escaping crazy Lipstick? Having a nap? Getting a manicure? Oh wait, you don't have fingers.

There are some things you just have to learn for yourself.

This is not Oz and I am not Dorothy.

Fine. I had things to do.

So what do you want? Why are you waking me up in the middle of the night? Am I still dreaming? Probably I am.

You're not. Believe me. But I need you to come and get me. I'm in the house. You know the one. And you know how to get in.

No! No! No! Where the heck are Star and Fish? Isn't this their job? I did what I set out to do. Sitting up, I stare into the darkness, my pulse racing double time.

But *maybe* I'm not done. Maybe saving Dad doesn't matter if the world we live in is about to be ruined by Lipstick and her EmoJabber zombie army. There are things I really like about this world. Like my dad. And Irma. And Jin. And Hannah. Even Zeus although he can be loud and annoying. And I like pottery and math class and Redwood. I like the way the air smells in San Francisco.

Maybe I really *do* have to save the world?

CHAPTER 41

RETURN TO THE SCENE OF THE CRIME

OH, I HATE THIS IDEA. I REALLY WANT TO STAY IN my bed and pretend that this is out of my hands. Finished. Done. But it's not and pretending otherwise is just putting off the inevitable. Before I can talk myself out of it, which won't take much, I'm out of bed. I pull on track pants and a hoodie, slip on tennis shoes, and shrug my backpack over my shoulders. I fling the rope ladder over the edge of my window and scramble down to the ground. One bus ride and thirty minutes later, I'm standing at the drainpipe, looking up at a balcony I really didn't think I would see again.

"If this was for anything less than saving the world," I

mutter, "I'd have stayed in bed." Gingerly, I place a foot on the lowest bracket securing the pipe and begin to climb. The upper part of the pipe is still detached from when Hannah almost fell, but if I center my gravity just so, I think I can make it before it peels away completely from the wall.

On the upside, I'm way faster than I was the first time. On the downside, I have no Frank. The minute I pass through the French doors, they will know I'm here. I land with an unpleasant thud on the balcony.

"I really thought we were through with each other," I mumble to the house. There is only one way I get in there and that is if the stupid stone helps me. I clear my head. I relax my shoulders.

Stone! Even unspoken, my tone is sharp, commanding. *You called me down here and now it is time for you to do my bidding.*

Look at you! You're getting the hang of this. I knew you would. Can't be all wishy-washy. Don't be afraid of your own voice.

Tell me where you are and make it so I can get there.

As you desire, my master. Just kidding. So you want to be invisible?

Yes.

Sorry. That's beyond my abilities, but I can make it so they don't see you.

Isn't that the same thing?

No. No it is not.

I am not going to stand here and argue with a magic stone. I have my limits. *Where are you?*

I'm in the kitchen.

At least I know where that is. *Okay. I'm coming.*

Oh goody!

I push open the French doors. If the stone is tricking me or is really not as talented as reported, I will soon be in big trouble. I push this from my mind and stride into the room. For a brief moment, I consider stuffing the headless snowman sculpture into my backpack just in case, but that does not seem like the best choice, all things considered. Out in the hallway, I sidestep the knight's armor still scattered across the floor and head for the stairs. No one comes. No pounding footsteps, no shouts of "Stop or else!" Just silence. It's like I'm not here.

Drifting up the stairs are voices that I recognize as Buzz's and Plaid's. Plaid admonishes Buzz for losing us down in the tunnels. "How could you leave them with their backpacks? What sort of idiot are you? This is a good gig and now you've gone and potentially ruined it."

"Hey," Buzz shoots back. "I got hit. It was not okay."

Plaid sighs loudly. "What am I going to do with you?"

I'm on the bottom step. They sit at the table, just yards from where I stand, the stone between them. My hands shake. I'm so nervous I might barf on my shoes. But I can't very well stand here like a statue forever.

I take a deep breath and step into the kitchen.

CHAPTER 42

INVISIBLE GIRL

I EXPECT BUZZ AND PLAID TO LEAP FROM THEIR chairs and grab me. I brace myself for impact. But they continue to argue about Buzz's level of stupidity in letting us blow up the cave door and escape. They don't even *turn* in my direction. A powerful surge of adrenaline rises in my veins. I creep closer, my feet as silent as a cat's. Buzz complains to Plaid that he is unsympathetic to the fact that Hannah clocked him in the head with the voice amplifier. Plaid says Buzz does not deserve sympathy, that he is hopeless and useless.

I stand right behind Plaid, as obvious as the nose on my face. But their eyes never drift in my direction. They are completely focused on each other. I am invisible.

Pretty cool, huh?

Oh yes. Very cool.

I slide around the edge of the table, now a simple arm's length from the stone. All I have to do is reach out and take it. Holding my breath, I snake my hand between Plaid and Buzz and close my fingers tight around the stone. They continue to argue. A surge of relief floods my system.

Got you.

So you have.

Slowly, I back away from the table. How long until the spell is broken and Plaid and Buzz realize the stone is gone? I inch backward toward the steps, keeping my eyes on them, but they just continue to argue. Finally, my feet bump the first step and I fly.

Moments later, I'm back on the balcony, panting. I shimmy onto the drainage pipe and begin to work my way back down. It's precarious, barely clinging to the wall. When I am about halfway down, it begins to buckle out from the wall. But I'm ready. I shove off as hard as I can and land dead center in the rosemary hedge, sure to keep my cast clear. I do a much better job falling this time. Scrambling to my feet, I slip between the hedges and out onto the street. Free and clear.

We did it!

Not bad.

Not bad? That was perfect. That was great! I wish I'd had you around the first time I broke into this house.

We can do many things together.

We can, can't we?

I'm so excited I can barely stand it. I feel powerful, invincible, and I want to tell everyone. I want to scream it from the rooftops. But there is no one to tell. All of San Francisco is sleeping.

By the time I crawl back through my bedroom window, there is an edge of light on the horizon. Clutching the stone, I slip under my covers and lay my head on the nice, cool pillow.

I *have* the stone. Think about what I could do. We could win the STEM fair! That would make Jin happy. Or maybe the three of us partner up and work on all the projects together? That would be fun, right? Even Dad says we make a good team.

Why not just win it yourself? Why share the glory?

Huh?

You heard me. You built Frank. Why should you share the spoils?

Because, well . . . they're my friends.

Are they? Isn't Jin just using you for a STEM fair victory he cannot secure himself?

No!

Are you sure?

My skin suddenly feels itchy and tight. Should I be sharing the credit for the STEM fair project when I did all the work? I'll be the one to rebuild Frank 3.0, just like I did with the last one, and I already have lots of improvements in mind. Do I owe Jin anything?

And Hannah tried to blackmail you. She just wants to control you. Why would you want that?

I . . . um . . . I don't know.

They are both using you.

I press my palms to my ears. I don't want to hear this.

All you have to do is decide you want to win that STEM fair and after that, everything is easy. Trust me.

Marvelous Merlin told me not to let the stone sway me, no matter what it offers. Don't give in, he said. I remember Jin grasping my hand when the rats swarmed us. I remember Hannah saving my life on the *Nebula*. The feeling I have when I'm with them is not made up. I know that in my heart. It's a place where I do not feel alone. All at once, I recognize the whiff of the underworld god Ördög.

He gave the stone the power to play on our worst instincts, our selfish insecurities.

And that's when I know the stone has got to *go*.

Quickly, I shove it under the comforter, as if that is going to help. Somehow the stone can sense my change of heart.

Really? You'd give up the chance to have it all? Your every desire fulfilled?

But the only reason I went back for the stone in the first place was to make sure Lipstick didn't use it to ruin a world I really like. I already have everything I want. I mean, sure, I'd like a kitten, but that's beside the point.

I know what you're trying to do. It won't work. Not on me.

I'm trying to help you. I thought you were the kind of person who understood that.

You thought wrong.

Giving EmoJabber a wide berth, I call Jin directly. He loops in Hannah. "Sorry to call so early on a Saturday," I say. "But we've got problems."

"Didn't we just solve our problems?" Jin asks.

"Lola probably made more." Hannah yawns.

"I went to the house," I blurt. "I have the stone. But we have to get rid of it. It's bad."

"What do you *mean* you have the stone?" Jin demands.

"Last night. I went back to the wedding cake mansion and took it." Even as I say the words, it feels like a dream, as if I might not have been there at all. "But it's dangerous and it needs to go."

Well, that's not very nice. I guess if you aren't going to appreciate the gifts I'm offering, I'll just give them to someone who will. Did you call her Lipstick?

Oh no. This is not good. "And, guys," I whisper, "we have to hurry."

CHAPTER 43

INTO THE DRINK

MY PLAN IS SIMPLE. CATCH A FERRY TO SAUSALITO, located on the other side of the bay. In the morning, they run pretty regularly. When we are halfway there, near the Golden Gate Bridge, I'll throw the stone overboard, where it will disappear into 350 feet of water, silenced forever, and no one will ever find it.

My friends want to know what's going on. I explain, leaving out the parts where the stone played on my worst instincts and almost convinced me it was right. "And I couldn't tell my dad. He'll just want to turn it over to Star and Fish and I don't trust those two at all. But we have to ditch it before it connects to Lipstick or we'll all be EmoJabber zombies."

"I don't want that." Hannah grimaces.

On the bus ride to the Ferry Building, not far from Pier 15, where the failed exchange occurred, Jin is rueful. "Too bad we never got to do cool magic stone stuff. That would have been fun." He doesn't understand the stone is here on earth to cause chaos, as was Ördög's desire. But I don't want to explain how I know that, so I smile.

"It's a bummer," I say. "I was thinking, though." And I have been, about lots of things, but mostly about how Jin, Hannah, and I were alone before and now we're not. It feels good not being alone anymore. And that's better than any magic.

"What have you been thinking?" Jin asks.

"About how with three brains we don't really need magic. What if *we* were a STEM fair team? Together?" Jin and Hannah stare at me as if I have a banana stuck in my ear or something. A warm spot forms in my belly. Am I pushing this friends/teamwork thing beyond its limits? I'm pretty new at it, so that's entirely possible. I wait, trying not to fidget.

"I think that's a great idea," Jin says after a long pause, swallowing hard.

Hannah tries for a casual shrug, but her eyes are bright. "I guess we work pretty well together. I mean, we've done some *stuff*." She giggles. "Redwood is going to freak. We're going to be unstoppable."

When we climb off the bus, we're hit with the heavy smell of seaweed and salt. The approaching ferry blasts its horn. The Ferry Building is crowded with tourists here for coffee and the Saturday-morning farmers' market. Quickly, we make our way to the boarding ramp, where we flash our student transport passes at a woman in a blue uniform, who waves us aboard.

On our way to the upper-level seating of the ferry, we pass a handful of passengers and none look familiar. No Lipstick. No Buzz or Plaid. This is good. We secure seats up top. No one wants to sit in the open air today. The fog still lingers, chilling the air.

I pull the stone from my pocket and study it. There are hints of green, but it doesn't glimmer like it did when I first found it, the moment it must have latched on to me, way back when we were on the *Nebula*. Down below, engines churn to life and the deck of the ferry vibrates. With the horn blowing, the boat pushes back from the pier and we head into the bay. The wind whips my hair around my head and my eyes water. It's hard to talk, so we just sit shoulder to shoulder and watch the Ferry Building recede in our wake, the skyline disappearing.

Will Dad let us stay in San Francisco, or will we be out on the road as soon as he gets his strength back up? I was so focused on finding him and getting back to my old life that I never considered what it would be like to leave my new one. A knot forms in my stomach.

Cut it out, Lola. Right now I have a job to do and that is to throw this stupid stone overboard so no one can ever get their hands on it again. I'm so busy telling myself to focus that I don't notice someone has taken the seat beside me. Jin's eyes go wide.

"Uh-oh." Hannah jumps to her feet.

The scent of orange cuts through the salty air.

And just like that, my heart surges. I want to squeeze my eyes shut and pretend none of this is happening, but that won't change things. Lipstick will still be seated beside me, grinning like the cat who ate the canary. Sorry, Zeus. No offense.

I react quickly, cocking my arm to hurl the stone into the frothy ocean, but Lipstick is faster. She grabs my wrist mid-throw and peels the stone from my hand.

"Nice try." She clutches the stone in a tight fist. "But the stone is done with you. It wants *me* now. You two, don't move."

But the stone's magic is intoxicating and she can't peel her eyes from it. Jin and Hannah slide around behind her.

I think they have a plan. Or they are running away and leaving me here. I'll have to wait and see.

"Too bad you don't know the secret to make it work," I say sharply, wanting to keep her attention on me so she doesn't see my friends slip from their seats. This works like a charm.

Fully behind her now, Jin and Hannah gesture wildly. I think they are telling me to buy time. Right. On it.

"I could make your life complicated," she says, "if you don't tell me."

"Jeez, lady," I say with a sigh. "My life is complicated already. Talk about not having any power. You should try being a kid these days. Nobody listens to kids. You get used to it after a while." Whatever they're plotting back there, I hope they hurry. "You already have power. Why do you need more? Why do you need to brainwash the world with EmoJabber? Why not do something good instead? You know, helpful?"

"I don't remember asking for your opinion," she says. She can't pull her gaze from the stone. It's like I'm barely there. Is it talking to her right now? Whispering in her ear? Is it offering her everything she wants and more? In a moment she will have the power to convince me to jump up on the ferry railing and squawk like a seagull. Whatever

Jin and Hannah are doing, it has to be *now*. "You should go home. Count yourself lucky you got your father back in one piece. Isn't that what you wanted?"

In the beginning, yes, but things have changed. Now I need to save the world.

"Unfortunately," I say, "the situation is not what it was."

Her eyes shift to me, glaring. "If you know what's good for you, you'll forget all about the stone. I have people watching your house. Don't think I won't ring that ridiculous bird's neck to make a point if I have to."

Oh, now she's being really mean. "You leave Zeus out of it," I growl. Just as those words leave my lips, Jin leaps forward and shoves Lipstick to the side, where she collides with Hannah, who hip-checks her hard enough that the stone flies from her hands. In a flash, I snatch it from the air, holding on tight.

The stone is warm in my hands, iridescent green, glowing. It tugs at the edges of my consciousness. Should I really toss it in the water, never to be seen again? The stone has important historical value. Shouldn't it be studied? Shouldn't it be on display in a museum or something? Is this a choice I'm really willing to make? Lipstick is regaining her footing.

And suddenly Jin and Hannah are beside me.

"Throw the stone, Lola. Let it go." Jin is calm, his voice confident. All his self-doubt is gone.

"We don't need it," Hannah says. "We are fine just as we are." Her eyes sparkle. She's not budging an inch.

Their words needle into my thoughts, pushing the lure of the stone out of the way. They are right. We don't need magic. We can make things happen all on our own. We just have to try.

I wind up like a pitcher on the mound and throw the stone as hard as I can. It sails in a perfect arc before hitting the water with an insignificant splash. Lipstick howls with pain and it's not from skinned knees. Kicking off her shoes, she climbs up on the ferry railing. It's a pretty big jump, but that doesn't stop her. She leaps into the water after the stone.

The three of us stand at the rail and watch with awe as she swims frantically toward the splash zone of the stone. But it's long gone, sunk deep into the muck at the bottom of the bay. Pandemonium breaks out when one of the crew spots Lipstick frantically diving below the waves, again and again. There's lots of screaming and running around. Someone throws a rescue buoy.

But Jin, Hannah, and me, we just stand there, grinning, and watch the chaos.

CHAPTER 44

STAR AND FISH HAVE PROBLEMS.

IN THE DAYS THAT FOLLOW, THERE ARE LOTS OF questions to which I give unsatisfying answers. Apparently, Star and Fish find my insistence that the stone had a bad attitude to be obstinate. My father is disappointed I tossed the stone overboard, although he tries not to show it.

"I would have liked to study it. I think we could have learned a great deal by having that opportunity."

But there is no point in describing to him what it was like to have the stone whisper in my ear. Or how as it got comfortable with me, it found darkness to exploit. It wanted to turn me rotten. Sure, we might have learned great things from it, but the risk was too high. Star and

Fish grumble, but I don't regret my decision. In some situations, adults cannot be trusted to do the right thing.

Like Lipstick. She wanted to be heard and no one would listen. I know a little bit about what that kind of desperation feels like and how easily a person can erase lines she swore she would never cross. I mean, I became an art thief! I was terrible at it, but still, I was willing to try anything.

And what would my path have been had I *succeeded*, made it out of the wedding cake mansion with the ballerinas intact? This thought makes me uneasy. It means Lipstick and I are not that different. In her shoes, I might have ended up just like her, isolated and alone.

But I'm not alone. Not anymore.

As Dad has decided to let us stay on at Great-Aunt Irma's for a while longer, at least until he is feeling right enough to go back out on the road, I am now a very ordinary Redwood student. I have channeled all the energy I spent on finding Dad into trying to win the STEM fair with my three-brain team. I really want to go to NASA summer camp. If they take us up in the reduced-gravity aircraft, I have vowed not to puke.

On a damp Tuesday in March, six weeks out from the STEM fair, Jin, Hannah, and I stop for milkshakes on the way to Jin's house. We have a work session scheduled to get Frank 3.0, Spy Goggles 2.0, and Noise Muffler 4.0 (please don't ask) in tip-top shape for competition. My friends bubble with ideas, everything from new power sources to better lenses to wireless earbuds to cuter bunny ears. I like to listen to them talk. It makes me think that I have found a lot of lost things lately, some that I didn't even know I was missing.

We are deep in a debate about how to present our projects, possibly as a tool set for those who are searching for something that has gone missing, when we notice two figures looming in the fog ahead. As we draw closer and they come into focus, I give a start. Star and Fish? I don't know what they are doing out here, but there's no way it's a coincidence. They wear their trademark black suits and dark sunglasses despite the fact there is no sun anywhere today. Hands clasped behind their backs, they stand at attention waiting for us to approach.

The last time I saw them, they were leaving Great-Aunt Irma's house in a huff because I refused to provide details on what it felt like to communicate with the stone. I believe they said I was being a brat. If they are seeking me out for another try, they will be disappointed. I steel myself for an unpleasant encounter.

"Is that who I think it is?" Jin's eyebrows spike.

"Oh yeah."

"Friends." Star offers a wide awkward grin. It's easy to pick out people who have no experience with kids and possibly were never kids themselves. Star and Fish fit the bill. "Imagine running into you here."

"I live right there," Jin says flatly.

"Don't even bother with a cover story," Hannah adds.

"I already told you everything I know," I say. We're out of the magical artifact recovery business. We are busy people. We have STEM fair projects to perfect if we are going to win. "I have nothing else to add. There's no point in asking. You're just wasting your time."

Star stretches that awkward grin clear across his face. Sometime in the last few weeks he's grown a mustache. It sits like a droopy caterpillar on his upper lip. "Actually, we aren't here about the stone at all." Fish nods in enthusiastic agreement.

"Well, then what do you want?" I'm uneasy. There is no way they are here to bust me because I haven't done anything. I have been the perfect student since Dad came home.

"It's very convenient to find all three of you together." Fish is also grinning widely and weirdly. Star and Fish are never this happy. Something is definitely up.

"You better just spill it," I suggest.

"We like to think the experiences with the stone were sort of a test for you young people." Star's grin falters a bit, but he pushes on. "You proved you have what it takes to assist the Task Force in its very important work."

"Sort of a *test*?" I eye him skeptically. No way. Their mission to find the Stone of Istenanya went totally off the rails and they were just lucky we persevered and saved the world.

"Well, fine," Star grumbles. "It wasn't really a test, not a planned one anyway, but it *could* have been. In any case, it seems we have a situation."

"A delicate situation," Fish clarifies. "Do you kids know about Pegasus?"

"From Greek mythology?" Where this is going, I really can't say.

"The flying horse?" Jin asks.

Star sighs. "Yes. That one."

Hannah steps forward. "What about him?" In the past, I would have found this conversation strange but not so much anymore. I have *seen* things.

"Pegasus supposedly wore a jeweled necklace," Fish says, "bestowed upon him by a minor goddess who I guess liked horses."

Goddesses? The last time we messed with a goddess's work, things got a little out of hand. Jin nudges me and waggles his eyebrows. Hannah grins. "Remember when I said there would be more adventures?"

I cross my arms against my chest defensively. "I've never heard of Pegasus wearing a necklace. And I've read a lot of mythology."

Star gives an apologetic shrug. "Surprisingly enough, there is an ancient text that describes the necklace. It seems thousands of years ago, during a long drought, the necklace was discovered along a stretch of parched Nile riverbed. The Pharaoh took possession and the necklace was passed down from dynasty to dynasty until it was lost."

"And?" My stomach tightens.

Fish jumps in. "There has been chatter about it, on our networks. Developments."

"Are these the same networks that the Shadow used to trick you? Forgive me if I'm skeptical."

"We've beefed up security," Star says quickly. "Created redundancies. Instituted encryption. Trust us. It's safe." I snort. Trust them? Never.

"A number of agents have been looking for the necklace," Fish says. "But success has been elusive."

"The boss says we might need a new perspective."

Star's nose crinkles up as if something stinks. "A different approach to the search."

"You want us to find Pegasus's necklace?" Jin blurts.

"We're going to be on the *Task Force*?" Hannah claps her hands with delight.

"You'd be honorary members," Fish clarifies, mopping her sweaty brow with a sleeve.

"Supplemental," adds Star.

"Extra help."

"Fresh eyes."

"Temporary."

Jin casts me a sideways glance. "They want us to be on the Task Force." He smirks. "Because they can't find stuff on their own. That's cool."

"Okay," says Hannah. "Let's say we agree. What do we get out of it?"

This question perplexes Fish. "You get to save the world. I thought that would be obvious."

"Do we get school credit? First-class airfare? Our choice of meals? Special Task Force passports?"

"I guess?"

Hannah grins. "Excellent! This is so *fun*. I'm in."

"Wait just a minute," I say. Have my friends already forgotten our experience with the Stone of Istenanya? What is wrong with them? Saving the world was supposed to be a one-off. I did not intend to make it my life's work. Still. Pegasus's necklace. "Before we agree to *anything*, you need to answer one question."

"Ahem . . . well . . . okay, I guess," says Star.

"If I were to put this necklace on, what *exactly* would happen?"

Fish swallows hard. "You could fly."

You have *got* to be kidding me.

ACKNOWLEDGMENTS

I REMEMBER SEEING *RAIDERS OF THE LOST ARK* when I was a kid and instantly falling in love, and not just with Indiana Jones. How did the storytellers weave action, adventure, humor, and characters that felt so real into a single tapestry? I had no idea (I was twelve), but I was hooked.

Later in life, when I had this ridiculous idea that I would write books, I wanted to serve up the same ingredients to readers that I had so loved in *Raiders*. Sure, the stakes are high, but we can have fun all the same, can't we?

I hope you enjoy Lola's adventures. I hope she makes your heart beat a little faster and makes you laugh. I'm already itching to get on the ride again.

There are a few people without whom this book (or any of my books!) would not see the light of day. Leigh

Feldman of Leigh Feldman Literary, who always has my back; Alyson Heller, a superhero of an editor who regularly saves me from falling into holes I have no hope of ever escaping; and the various lovely middle-grade authors it has been my pleasure to meet over this past year, including those wild and crazy Renegades of Middle Grade. You know who you are.

I suddenly have kids in junior high and high school. Gone are the days when I could conduct reader research on the friends innocently coming to our house to play. But I'm oh so proud of what these kids are growing into. They are awake and aware and ready to light the way for the rest of us. Max and Katie, thank you for being brave. As always, I am cheering for you from the sidelines.

As I write this, my brother is battling cancer. I truly believe that somewhere out there is a kid who will uncover the answer and beat back this very real demon. Maybe this kid is even reading *Lola Benko, Treasure Hunter* right now.

And lastly, this book is for Mike, my cheerleader, always willing to lend me some of his faith when mine runs dry. I am lucky and grateful to be on this journey with you. Steady on.

TURN THE PAGE FOR A PEEK AT LOLA'S NEXT ADVENTURE!

LOLA BENKO,
TREASURE
HUNTER

THE MIDNIGHT MARKET

Beth McMullen

Author of the MRS. SMITH'S SPY SCHOOL FOR GIRLS series

BLAME THE FLYING HORSE

It's been exactly three months since a mythical flying horse and his stupid bejeweled necklace ruined my life. Yes. You heard that right. Things were going *fine*. We had saved the famous globe-trotting, treasure-hunting archaeologist Lawrence Benko, who is also my dad. Better yet, I no longer had to live out of a suitcase while I followed him around on his crazy adventures. I had my own room, plastered with cute kitten posters, at Great-Aunt Irma's place. I went to an okay school (as far as schools go), but, most importantly, I had *friends*. Real ones! Friends are not easy to make and keep when you're living out of a suitcase. Like I said, everything was *fine*. But in zooms the flying horse, who rudely stomps all over my life, reminding me I am nothing special.

For any of this to make sense, let's backtrack a year to the botched burglary of a valuable statue. I would never have entered the thieving business, except my father was *missing*. Everyone said he was dead, but knowing that was impossible, I was intent on finding him. However, a search and rescue mission required resources I didn't have. Enter the ugly statue of spindly ballerinas worth a *million* bucks, which would have funded my exploits for quite some time . . . until I broke it with my butt falling out a window.

They could have sent me to the slammer for crimes committed against my fellow citizens *and* innocent works of art, but instead the judge decided on a different sort of punishment. I was enrolled at Redwood Academy, a fancy private school in the Presidio. It was to be my second chance (or third or fourth or fifth, but who's counting?) to be a good law-abiding citizen. But Redwood turned out not to be any sort of punishment at all. At Redwood, I met my best friends, Jin and Hannah, and it's a good thing I did because life got *so* much more interesting when they showed up.

Together (kind of by accident, if I'm being honest), we discovered that my father had been kidnapped by an insane person who wanted help finding and using the Stone of Istenanya, a magical rock from an old Hungarian folktale, which was not supposed to exist. But the rock turned out to be *real*. (Believe me, we were surprised too.) And to make matters worse, whoever possessed it had the power of mind control. Not okay, especially when you factor in that insane person I mentioned. We called her "Lipstick," and she was pretending to be a supernice, generous billionaire tech genius named Benedict Tewksbury (actually, she *was* a tech genius and a billionaire, but she was *not* nice). Her goal was to use a chat app she'd invented called EmoJabber, along with the stone, to control the minds of all her chatting minions. Had she succeeded, it would have been a real problem.

But she didn't! We stopped Lipstick, rescued my dad, and retrieved the stone. Yes, you heard that right. We *saved* the world. Sometimes when you are a kid, you feel like things are happening *to* you, without your permission or anyone even asking your opinion. It doesn't matter if you yell or scream or protest—the adults get the only vote. When we were treasure hunting the stone, however, it was the complete opposite. *We* were making things happen.

But then I threw the stone into the San Francisco Bay and everyone got really mad at me, especially Lipstick.

In my defense, that stone was bad news and humanity doesn't always make good choices. All you have to do is look at history to know that.

In the process of saving the world, I discovered a few things. First, I *like* having friends. It gives me a buzzy feeling inside that is hard to explain. And second, my father works, on occasion, for the International Task Force for the Cooperative Protection of Entities with Questionable Provenance. I know! What a name! Don't even try to say it when you are sleep-deprived. Your tongue will end up in knots. Called the ITFCPEQP for short (not much of an improvement, if you ask me), the Task Force hunts for artifacts that might possess qualities "uncommon on earth." You know, magical stuff that is not supposed to exist, things that us flawed humans can potentially find and use to make a mess of things. Dad says if you give people unexpected otherworldly power, they go berserk. Us humans like to believe the world is a certain way, and if suddenly that's not true, things get complicated. The Task Force is meant to stop the chaos before it happens.

I'm not inclined to argue with him after seeing what happened when the Stone of Istenanya turned out to be real. But I did argue that he never should have kept his Task Force treasure hunting a secret for, well, let's see, *my entire life.* He apologized all over himself, but only later did I realize he never promised he wouldn't do it again.

Parents. What are you going to do?

So there we were, world-saving, fearless-in-the-face-of-evil rock stars. But what next? Once you get a taste for missing magical mythical potentially dangerous treasure hunting, you cannot go back to the life of an ordinary middle school student for all the doughnuts in the world. And let me be clear, I love doughnuts.

Of course, that was the exact moment Agents Star and Fish, Task Force treasure hunters, swooped in and asked us to come on board as honorary, temporary, supplemental members, specifically to help find *another* treasure.

And that was *just* the opening the flying horse and his fancy jewelry needed to ruin my life.

IT DEPENDS ON YOUR POINT OF VIEW

It's day sixteen of summer vacation. It was supposed to be a summer of treasure hunting and having outrageous amounts of fun. Instead, me, Jin, and Hannah are tucked into the Maker Lab, a tiny studio behind Jin's San Francisco house, created with loving care by his mom, who apparently likes to build robots when she can't sleep. The lab is chock-full of unbelievable stuff for inventing things. And, occasionally, blowing them up. But usually that part is unintentional.

We are the team that won the STEM fair grand prize back in March with an ugly yet powerful electromagnetic pulse device that effectively scrambles anything that requires electricity or a communication signal. But since the Pegasus disaster, we are all wrong. Dad says I should stop calling it a disaster.

"Change your point of view," he keeps saying. "Look at it as a *situation*, a learning opportunity." Maybe, but this is the first time I've seen Hannah since school ended more than *two weeks ago*, so I'm thinking more disaster and less situation.

Hannah is draped across the couch, making spitballs and launching them at Jin, who, in turn, is sucking helium out of a balloon and saying all of Yoda's best lines from *Star Wars*. I dragged everyone here today because we are supposed to come up with new ideas for the regional STEM competition, right around the corner, but instead we are spitballing and Yoda-ing.

And I do mean *dragged*. Before Pegasus, we could not wait to hang out together. We were treasure hunters! We were a team! Now Hannah is obsessed with adrenaline, adventure, and *Bodhi*, and Jin is obsessed with Paul, Paul, and *Paul*. I'm a total afterthought, a discarded toy that used to be fun but now is a drag. When I think about it, it clogs up my throat and I can't swallow right.

"You guys!" I bark from my seat at the wide worktable, tapping my watch face for emphasis. "Time is passing!

Brainstorm! Exciting solutions to our problem of what to make for the competition include . . . GO!"

Jin sucks in some helium. "Can I leave yet?" he asks, sounding a lot like Minnie Mouse. "I have to meet Paul for Minecraft in four minutes." Paul. Ugh.

Aiming her spitball straw at my head, Hannah concurs. "I'm meeting Bodhi at the climbing gym. It's a speed work-day. We think we want to free solo El Cap in Yosemite. That would be wild, right?"

Her eyes sparkle in anticipation and my heart sinks. This is not my first attempt to bring us back together, but my friends have *new* friends that are somehow better. Paul is Jin's old best friend who ghosted him when he moved to New York. I mean, he disappeared, vanished, poof, gone without a trace.

But right after we won the STEM competition, Paul reappeared. He sent Jin this woven friendship bracelet embedded with a tiny computer-chip charm, the kind of thing you are forced to make at summer camp, and Jin loves it more than anything, even cake or his little brother. But it's just an ugly bracelet, not an apology or a promise to do better! After the bracelet, Paul started texting Jin as if nothing had happened, as if no time had passed, and everything was exactly as it was, except the geography.

And Jin defends him, like he's been brainwashed. According to Jin, Paul was going through a "transition" when he went radio silent. It was really hard for Paul to move away, and his new private school, Chappaqua Prep or Chadwick or Cheesehead or whatever, was socially tough and he needed time to get his feet on the ground, blah, blah, blah.

But *why* would you take back a friend who has treated you badly, especially when you have better options right in front of you? Unless those options suddenly don't seem so good? Maybe I'm missing something, but I don't think I'd want to be friends again with someone who pretended I was dead.

And don't get me started on the boyfriend Bodhi! Hannah met him at the climbing gym, where she began hanging out right after the Pegasus disaster . . . I mean, *situation*. She can't go very long without doing something thrilling or she gets cranky, and we were obviously much too boring. I mean, she didn't say that exactly, but we got it.

And we know Bodhi is her boyfriend because she makes sure to remind us at every opportunity. Of course, that would be much more annoying if we *ever* saw her. Which we don't. Bodhi has filled her calendar with an array of thrilling adventures—rock climbing, whitewater rafting, scuba diving in Monterey, backpacking the Sierra Nevada—all sorts of thrills I cannot hope to match. Apparently, Bodhi belongs to a family of thrill seekers and adrenaline junkies who have welcomed Hannah with open arms. Or something like that.

Sure, Bodhi is nice enough and hangs on Hannah's every word. And he has an enviable head of curly hair and rich dark eyes and cruises around San Francisco on a long board, which makes him . . . something, I guess. He even took Hannah on a date to the Japanese Tea Garden in Golden Gate Park, and they shared a pot of tea and it was *so* romantic. Barf. But I can't like him because he's completely replaced us. I'm not sure Jin has even noticed, but I sure have.

It's bad. I can't even lure Jin and Hannah to the ice-cream shop, and they both would sell their own mothers up the river for a good cone. I have nothing to offer that compares with Paul or Bodhi. We aren't treasure hunters. We aren't a team. It occurs to me, not for the first time, that we aren't best friends anymore either.

And I blame Pegasus. You know the one I'm talking about, mythical winged horse, Zeus's sidekick, eventually tamed by Athena, the goddess of war. What you might *not* know is that Athena gave Pegasus a necklace. Maybe because Pegasus favored sparkly bling or maybe it was more like a collar with a tag—*If you find this horse, please send him home to Mount Olympus*. But the point is that the necklace is not supposed to exist, and yet, as seems to happen lately with alarming frequency, it *does*.

When the necklace suddenly appeared on the Task Force's radar, Star and Fish were put on the mission. As it turns out, if a human wears the necklace, she can *fly*. The necklace needed to be found fast, before someone ended up as the lead story on the local news and there was pandemonium. People don't react well to the unexpected. Again, I refer you to history.

But finding the necklace wasn't so easy. All of Star and Fish's hot leads went cold. They spun in circles, chasing their tails. And the more they struggled, the more panicky they got. They needed a win. Desperate, they called us. We had found the Stone of Istenanya with only our wits. Imagine what we could do with *actual* resources behind us? They bet on us working our magic twice.

And being honorary, temporary, supplemental members of the Task Force was great! It was everything we imagined. Excellent snacks! Lightning-fast computers! First-class airfare! Not only that, but finding the necklace turned out to be no big deal. Seriously. *That* part was easy.

There is a reason why kids make the best treasure hunters. Adults are stuck in one point of view, and once it solidifies, they cannot see all the gray between the black and white. Changing your point of view is critical if your job is to consider the fantastical.

Jin interrupts my thoughts. "Ow!" He pulls back his hand.

"Huh?"

Jin points down at the circuit I've been carelessly welding, unaware of a long tail of wire coiled right up to where Jin's hands rest on the table. "You electrocuted me!"

"Sorry," I say quickly. "I was thinking."

"About electrocuting me?" Jin blows his floppy bangs out of his eyes.

"Not exactly."

We started our hunt with Jin's idea to dig deep into social media posts about flying people. Yup. And with the computer power we suddenly had at our disposal, it didn't even take very long. Star and Fish lingered around us, offering advice and tips, but mostly we ignored them. Team LJH had this totally under control. We were going to be legends. Bigger than Phoenix and Gryphon, but without the, you know, murder and insanity part.

In less than two weeks, Jin found a boy in Rome who swore he'd seen a man soaring above the Coliseum. For real! Wild, right? Once we made contact with the boy, we grabbed the thread and followed it from lead to lead, post to post, kid to kid, until we uncovered Amira, a woman who sold housewares at a charming outdoor market in Marrakesh, Morocco, a small African country across the Strait of Gibraltar from Spain. In addition to pots and pans and plastic storage containers, Amira would sell the occasional magical artifact, a trade she had learned from her father, apparently.

And Amira had the *necklace*. She intended to take it to the next Midnight Market because that is how it is done in the magical-object world of commerce. But as soon as she got over the fact that a bunch of middle school kids had figured out her secret, she was willing to make a deal. After all, with the full backing of an enormous global agency, we had *resources*.

We were Morocco-bound within hours, our freshly printed Task Force passports, with the purple cover and the gold lettering, clutched in our hands. Things were happening. We all agreed this was our destiny, what we were meant to do with our lives. It was totally fun.

When we arrived at Amira's market stall as planned,

she claimed she did not have the necklace with her because she expected us the next day. "Come back tomorrow with the payment," Amira told us, "and the necklace is yours." She even offered to throw in some knockoff Adidas sneakers as a gesture of goodwill.

We should have known something was up. We should have seen the signs. We had a deal and now that deal had changed. Sure, it was a minor hiccup, but as Dad would say, the devil is in the details. And we were too full of ourselves to notice.

Hubris is one of those words that sounds like what it means. Excessive pride or self-confidence. In other words, believing there is no *way* you can fail. The necklace practically in our hands, with victory all but assured, we made the mistake of reporting our success to Star and Fish. We told them we *had* the necklace.

Without verifying, which is kind of their fault, Star and Fish turned around and told everyone in the treasure-hunting universe that the necklace was secure. There would be no more trouble from flying mortals. They were so excited by their own brilliance in using us that they even told the big bosses. And the big bosses told the presidents and the prime ministers. The presidents and prime ministers said "Yay!" and agreed to continue funding the

Task Force forever and ever. Mission accomplished.

But it *wasn't*.

When we returned the next morning, with the sun beginning to rise, Amira politely informed us a better offer had materialized and, being as she was a businesswoman, she took that offer. The necklace was *gone*. She didn't even apologize. This shocking new reality came with the distinct sensation that we'd been *had*. And as it turns out, I was right. Lipstick was paying us back for stealing the Stone of Istenanya from her and throwing it into the San Francisco Bay. She wanted us to know how failure felt. And now we did.

Star and Fish had to unravel the whole mess, and at the bottom of the mess was us. As quasi team leader, I tried to take the blame. But Star and Fish were humiliated and angry, and all heads had to roll.

We were immediately dismissed, fired, uninvited, kicked off, left at the curb, abandoned, disowned, disavowed. It was *over*. My friends drifted away to other things, to Paul, to Bodhi. Our team dissolved.

I don't know how long I've been lost in my thoughts, but from the look on Hannah's face, it's too long. And I've probably been mumbling to myself too. Great.

She waves at me. "I *said* we're going. Me and Jin. You can

stay if you want. To put Frank's face back on or whatever."

"You guys are *leaving*?" I bleat pathetically. "But what about regionals? We don't even have an idea."

Jin glances up from texting and shrugs. "Maybe we skip regionals," he says.

"*Skip* the regionals?" I'm aware my voice has gone squeaky and a little desperate.

Jin throws up his hands. "I mean, we don't have a project and we're not really into it. I'm just putting the possibility out there. Don't freak out."

Oh, I'm beyond freaking out. Freaking out is for amateurs. I'm in full-on catastrophic meltdown mode. I clench my teeth so hard I'm surprised they don't shatter.

Hannah, refusing to meet my eyes, mutters something about Bodhi waiting at the gym, collects her stuff, and waves a vague goodbye. Jin, thumbs still flying, leaves for his Minecraft game with Paul. Before they go, neither Jin nor Hannah mentions when we should next get together to work on our STEM project or just to hang out.

And that leaves me alone in Jin's backyard, staring at a mangled Frank 4.0, as if he might hold the answers to my problems. But he has nothing to say, so I shrug on my backpack and head for home. My throat is tight, my eyes threaten to spill tears, and worst of all, I'm out of ideas, a completely foreign experience for me. Maybe it's time to bring this problem to Dad? He claims to be an excellent out-of-the-box thinker, and right now the box I'm in feels bottomless.